Demon Hunters 7: Extrication

Demon Hunters 7: Extrication

Avril Sabine

Cracked Acorn Productions
Australia

Demon Hunters 7: Extrication

Published by

Cracked Acorn Productions

PO Box 1365

Gympie, Queensland 4570

Australia

978-1-925617-96-2 (Kindle)

978-1-925617-97-9 (EPUB)

978-1-925617-98-6 (Print)

Genre: Young Adult Urban/Fantasy/Horror

For my parents. For all three of them. I'm lucky to have had so many and that they have encouraged me in my dreams.

Esther is determined to change her life around. To stop mourning, stop being angry and most of all to stop getting into fights. She decides it's going to take a new attitude, a new city and a new job. As always, things don't go according to plan and she's left wondering who will mourn her if the worst happens?

*

This story was written by an Australian author using Australian spelling.

Name Pronunciation

Like many names there is more than one way to pronounce the following ones. These are the pronunciations used in this story.

Dazreyella (daz-rey-ella)

Elvera (el-vera)

Esther (es-ter)

Jerusha (jer-roo-sha)

Malachi (mal-ah-kye)

Nethod (neth-od)

Talitha (tah-lee-thah)

Torrnon (tore-non)

Chapter One

Esther stepped off the bus, remaining on the grassed footpath while it drove away. She wiped the palms of her hands against her knee length, black skirt as she watched the bus disappear around the corner. The day was a little cool, being that it was late May, but not so cold that she needed to wear a jumper and long pants. Which was a good thing since her only option would have been worn jeans and faded jumpers.

After wiping her hands against the skirt once more, she took a folded piece of paper from the handbag she'd picked up recently at an op shop for a couple of dollars. She couldn't very well have turned up at the interview using her backpack as a handbag. She opened the piece of paper and stared at the address. Her stomach did a long, slow turn.

What was she thinking? No experience required didn't mean they'd be interested in someone who'd just turned eighteen for a personal assistant. She halted the negative thoughts that began to form. Things would be different. She straightened her shoulders and slipped the piece of paper back into the handbag.

A new town, well technically a city, hopefully a new job, and no one here that knew her past. Or at least the parts of it she didn't want to share. Yet she continued to stand where she was, trying to convince herself to take another step forward.

She'd spent an hour braiding her plain brown hair back from her face, applying a light dusting of makeup and choosing what to wear from her limited wardrobe, all done in the bathroom at the bus terminal. Luckily her clothes didn't need to be ironed and the creases had fallen out when she shook them after taking them from her backpack. She'd chosen a green blouse the sales assistant had told her made her hazel eyes look almost green. Which had to be better than their usual murky colour.

Her resume was neatly typed and in a folder she'd put in the spacious handbag. All she had to do was walk down the street to the house where the interview was being held and lie convincingly. She'd had plenty of practice at lying over the years. To teachers, foster parents and occasionally the police.

Yet this felt different. Important. Without this job, her only option would be to return to Morayfield and move back in with her uncle and cousins she'd lived with since finishing year twelve last November. They'd been just as unhappy to have her turn up unexpectedly on the doorstep, as she'd been to arrive there.

Esther forced herself to head down the street. She couldn't stand where she was all afternoon. Besides ending up late for the interview, this looked like the kind of neighbourhood where people would object to strangers standing out the front of their homes.

Walking under a fig tree she felt the ridges of the roots beneath the thin soles of her slip-on shoes. She couldn't have worn her scuffed boots. They hadn't looked fancy enough for a personal assistant. Doubts hit her again. She wasn't fancy enough to be a personal assistant.

Her steps slowed as she approached a paved driveway leading to the door of the two storey house. The front of the building was filled with large glass doors that although capable of being opened, led nowhere. Fancy iron railings prevented anyone from stepping outside. There were two on either side of the large, double timber entrance doors that were set in the middle of the building and another two above each of them. Curtains were drawn back at the glass doors and she caught glimpses of antique furniture.

What had she been thinking? A job requiring no experience and providing room and board might sound great, but she had no hope of getting it. As one of her earlier foster parents would have said, her expectations of the world were unrealistic. As she headed for the door, her steps slowed further and she was nearly at a standstill.

The door swung open and a young man stepped out, glaring at a broad-shouldered man in a suit. "I could do the job as good as any female. Maybe better."

The broad-shouldered man crossed his arms over his chest. "The ad was specific. Females only may apply. Elvera would not feel comfortable having a young man stay in the house with her of an evening."

"I wouldn't-"

The man interrupted. "You may go."

With a glare, the young man strolled down the driveway. He barely glanced at Esther.

The broad-shouldered man remained in the doorway. "Are you the two o'clock appointment?"

Nodding, Esther hurried forward. "Sorry. I'm a little early."

The man looked past her. "I'd say you're right on

time since the one thirty appointment has already ended." He stepped back out of the doorway and gestured for her to enter.

She resisted the urge to wipe her hands against her skirt again. Her palms felt damp and her stomach once again did a long, slow turn. "Thank you." She entered the house, the pale, timber floorboards of the foyer smooth and hard beneath her shoes.

"This way, please."

She looked upwards as she followed him further into the house. A fancy, wrought iron railing, which matched the railing of the stairs on her left, edged the open section of the floor upstairs. All she could see from this angle were carpeted hallways. They entered a set of doors directly ahead, stepping around the timber table and heading to the right where two three-seater lounge suites were set along two sides of a coffee table.

A woman sat in the middle of the lounge suite that faced the direction of the front of the house. She appeared to be in her late thirties and her long black hair was a single length, brushed back from her face to cascade down her back. Her makeup, like her dress, was elegant and understated and her dark eyes examined Esther.

"Your two o'clock appointment is early, Elvera."

The woman inclined her head. "Thank you, Norman. That will be all for now." Her gaze remained on Esther. She gestured to the other lounge suite. "Take a seat."

Before she sat down, Esther took the folder from her handbag and removed the resume, placing it on the coffee table in front of Elvera. She felt uncomfortable with the woman staring at her. "You have a beautiful house." The words felt lame the moment she'd spoken them.

"It's a contemporary take on the French Provincial style. Old world elegance with contemporary style and convenience." Elvera stared at her a moment longer before she picked up the resume and glanced over it. "Esther. A rather Biblical name."

She had no idea how to reply to that comment, so she remained silent. Something that more than one school guidance counsellor had suggested she do. Although they normally made that comment about her back answering.

"Is your family religious?"

Esther almost shrugged. The surroundings seem too elegant for something as simple as a shrug. "I'm an orphan."

"No extended family?"

She wasn't about to mention her uncle and cousins.

Especially since her oldest cousin had a police record. It wasn't like she planned to have anything further to do with them. That was if she could get this job. "I was placed with a foster family when I was eleven."

Elvera again glanced at the resume. "You have been with them the past seven years?"

"They relocated to another town and my caseworker decided it was best I stay in the area I was accustomed to and another foster family was found for me." She met Elvera's gaze. It was partly the truth. It was the comment her caseworker had made when her foster family had said there was no way they wanted her to go with them.

"And your current foster family? Are you close to them?"

She wanted to demand what any of this had to do with the job. Breathing out slowly, she frantically tried to come up with a suitable answer. "I finished with the foster system when I completed year twelve last year."

"Does that mean you no longer have anything to do with your last foster parents?"

Her foster parents had been the ones who were religious. They'd given her regular, sad looks and promised to pray for her. She nearly shrugged, her gaze momentarily drawn to the elegant surroundings.

"Taking in children is their calling. I moved out to make way for other children in need of a place to live."

"How very noble of them."

Not knowing if Elvera was being sarcastic, or if she was complimenting them, she remained silent. It probably was noble of them. They'd driven her crazy with their long-suffering looks and continual promises to pray for her. She hadn't needed their pity.

Elvera placed the resume on the coffee table. "Where have you been living since you moved out of their home and what have you been doing? You haven't listed a single job."

Again she made herself remain still when she would have preferred to shrug. "An acquaintance from school and her family needed someone to look after their house while they were overseas. They returned at the same time as I saw your ad so I emailed you regarding an interview." She tried to remain relaxed, smiling in an effort to help herself with that. "It's the first time I've been to Brisbane even though where I lived with them on the Sunshine Coast really isn't that far from here." She didn't bother mentioning the weeks she'd spent in Brisbane when she'd run away at thirteen. They didn't count. Nor the time she'd spent with her uncle and cousins in Morayfield.

Elvera studied her. "You have no family, no job history, and this is the first time you've been to Brisbane."

Her heart sank. This was it. Elvera was about to tell her she wasn't suitable. "The ad said experience wasn't necessary."

"Answer the question."

Her hands started to curl into fists at the tone Elvera used. She stopped them in mid-motion. "I have always had chores with each foster family I stayed with and my parents had no siblings." She wasn't about to count her mother's brother. Besides, he had only been her half brother. "And this is the first time I've been to Brisbane. I don't know the area or anyone here, but I'm sure I can find my way around quickly."

"No boyfriend to interrupt your time? Friends who will demand you attend social events with them?"

"No one."

Elvera looked her up and down. "I find that hard to believe. Are you honestly telling me you are completely alone in this world?"

She wanted a fresh start. That wouldn't happen if she dragged her old baggage with her. "I broke up with my boyfriend when he went south to Uni and my best friend moved to North Queensland with her family at the start of the year and we've drifted apart." Those lies seemed preferable to telling Elvera that her friend had been chosen for the amount of trouble she could cause and she'd been half-heartedly dating a boy who owned a motorbike because it annoyed her foster parents. Or at least it had caused those sorrowful looks of theirs. She'd never been able to get them to raise their voices in anger. No, she was the only one who'd given into anger. But not anymore. She was starting afresh.

"Stand up and turn around." Elvera made a movement with her hand to indicate spinning.

Esther didn't immediately move. When she did, she slowly turned, feeling awkward. What did this have to do with the job? She nearly blurted out the question.

"At least you're not ugly. Your lack of fashion can be fixed. Have you ever considered changing your name?"

Esther stared at Elvera, not sure she'd heard right. "My name?"

Elvera made a dismissive gesture with her hand. "Sit down. No need to tower over me like that."

Esther dropped onto the lounge suite. She barely

managed to bite back the words that wanted to escape. Elvera had been the one who'd told her to stand up.

"When can you start?" Elvera asked.

Esther opened her mouth. Not a single word came out.

"Surely it isn't that difficult a question."

"Now." She blurted the word out. "Or whenever suits you. I have no other commitments." She didn't have much of anything, not just commitments. But that would change. It was time to get on with her life and stop being angry at everything that had happened.

"If you let Norman know the address, he can collect your luggage for you." Elvera rose to her feet. "There is a full list of the services I use on the coffee table in the drawing room at the front of the house. Along with other details you will need." She started towards the doorway that led to the front of the house. "There will be no need for you to go upstairs." She glanced over her shoulder. "Don't sit there. Follow."

Chapter Two

Esther hurried after Elvera, dazed. She had the job?

"Your bedroom is here on the left." Elvera gestured towards the open door that was beyond a short hallway, two doors opening off each side of the hallway. "The drawing room is at the front of the house and anything you need to collect or leave for me to peruse can be left in the library opposite it."

Esther looked from one side of the foyer to the other, peering inside the two open doors. The drawing room, which was on her left, looked like a lounge room without a television and the library contained two comfortable looking armchairs placed around a small coffee table with bookcases along one wall. There was a scattering of ornaments on the shelves amongst the books.

"Do you have any questions?"

She didn't know if she could come up with a

coherent sentence let alone questions. "I'll read over the information first."

Elvera inclined her head. "A very good plan." She glanced at the front door. "Norman has a room above the garage out the back. You can either access it by going out the front door and around the side or through the back doors and across the patio."

"Thank you."

Once more Elvera inclined her head before striding towards the stairs and heading up them.

Esther stumbled inside the drawing room and dropped onto an armchair. She had the job? She'd been so certain she hadn't stood a chance. Particularly with all the questions Elvera had asked.

Her gaze was drawn to the coffee table in front of her. The only thing on it was a smartphone. She checked underneath it. Nothing. The phone contained the information? She turned it on. Laughter nearly escaped. Already her new life was nothing like her old one.

She scrolled through the details, frowning. It seemed like the job mainly consisted of letting Elvera know when it was time for her to attend various appointments and events. That was it? Surely the woman could have set alarms for that. She reached the end of the list. And running errands. How many errands could a person run in a day? She supposed she'd soon find out. Noticing there was a file asking for details like her bank account, she filled it in and sent it to the number listed below the questions.

"Elvera said your luggage needs to be collected."

Esther pressed a hand against her heart. Norman stood by the doorway of the drawing room. "I didn't hear you enter."

"The address?"

She looked him up and down. In his fitted suit, he'd be out of place at the bus terminal. "It's okay. I can collect it."

"Do you have money for a taxi?" Norman took out a leather wallet.

"That's okay I-" she broke off before she could tell him she'd catch the bus, her gaze fixed on the fifty dollar notes he took out. She tried again. "I can-"

Norman interrupted her, counting out two hundred dollars. "Elvera doesn't like to be bothered any more than necessary. Keep your receipts."

She stared at his retreating figure, holding the money in her outstretched hand. Was this normal? She lowered her hand. Maybe she should have stuck with continually getting fired from takeaway and fast food shops. At least she knew what to expect with them.

Straightening her shoulders, she slipped the money into her handbag. She could do this. She momentarily closed her eyes, trying not to remember the incident that had sent her into a panic, desperate for a new life.

The words hadn't been aimed at her. There'd been aimed at her cousin. The one with the police record. His girlfriend had been shouting at him, but her words had struck a chord with Esther. 'You're so busy being angry with the world and yelling at it, that the world is leaving you behind. Just like I am.' She'd strode away, only her words remaining behind. Her cousin had raced out the door after his ex-girlfriend while Esther had remained where she'd stood in the lounge room, the words echoing over and over in her mind. Her cousin hadn't been the only one angry at the world.

Pushing uncomfortable thoughts away, Esther slipped the phone into her handbag and strode to the bedroom Elvera had said she could use. She froze in the doorway. This was her room? She wasn't ready for this. How could anyone relax in such a room? Or sleep on the bed? She'd be terrified to mess it up. Her hand grasped the doorframe as she held on, trying not to think about what would happen when Elvera figured out she wasn't the person she pretended to be.

She thought of the clothes in her backpack. She

needed something better to wear. Her hand brushed against the handbag. Surely she could pick up a few clothes and return the money after her first paycheck.

The rest of the afternoon was taken up collecting her backpack from the bus terminal, where she'd paid for short term locker storage, and shopping for a handful of clothes. She washed them at a laundromat rather than return to Elvera's and ask about using the laundry. Did people go straight out and buy clothes the moment they got a job? She didn't know and didn't want to risk doing things that were out of the ordinary. She needed this job. The last thing she wanted to do was return to her uncle's place. And she was all out of options.

She had nearly arrived back at Elvera's house when a text message came through. It was a politely worded order to join Elvera for dinner at seven thirty. She checked the time. An hour and a half to get ready. That should be more than enough time.

It didn't end up being as much time as she'd thought it would be and she made it to the table with minutes to spare. Norman put a plate in front of each of them and opened a bottle of wine, pouring them a glassful.

Esther eyed the fancy food and glass of wine. "I don't much like the taste of wine."

Elvera raised her glass to her lips and had a sip, her gaze remaining on Esther. "You will like this one." She placed the glass on the table.

Esther stared at Elvera for a moment. That sounded like an order. She supposed there were worse things. She took a sip of the bitter drink, smiling and nodding her head. "It's actually not too bad." There were other things she would have preferred to say. But insulting her new boss' taste probably wasn't a good idea.

Elvera inclined her head. Her gaze remained on Esther a moment longer. "You need to go shopping tomorrow. Those clothes…" She looked Esther up and down. "Take Norman with you. He will purchase something more suitable." Again she looked Esther up and down. "It's obvious you need help choosing appropriate clothes."

Esther's grip tightened on her cutlery. She'd spent ages choosing this outfit. She lowered her gaze, shifting the food around on the plate in front of her rather than voice the objection that wanted to escape. Maybe this job wouldn't be as easy as she'd first thought.

"You can also organise an appointment at my salon. Your hair is in need of attention." Elvera paused a moment. "You had best tell them you need the full works. Your hands and nails are a mess. The details are in the phone I gave you. Tell them I sent you."

She slowly breathed out, keeping her gaze on her plate. "Thank you." Somehow she'd managed to keep the anger out of her voice. Did Elvera think everyone could afford to live like her?

The rest of the meal was silent and when she'd finish eating, Elvera rose to her feet. "Finish your food and wine. I'll see you for breakfast at seven."

Esther remained where she was, staring at the doorway Elvera had walked through. She assumed the woman had headed up the stairs, but she walked as softly as Norman. She slowly rose to her feet. There was no way she'd last long in this job. Eventually, she'd say something she shouldn't. She'd begin looking for another job next week. For now, she'd learn more about Brisbane and figure out where she'd like to work and live.

Finished the food and about to move away from the table, her attention was caught by the glass of wine. Worried Elvera might comment on her leaving so much of it after having insisted she would like the drink, Esther took it to the sink, along with the rest of the crockery and cutlery. She tipped the wine out, running water to get rid of the evidence. A smile formed. Her cousin would have been horrified at her wasting alcohol. Not that she'd tell him.

Her smile faded. She had no one she could tell anything to. Not about her day, and not about her plans. She strode to her room, pausing in the doorway. She didn't belong here. Eventually, she'd find the place she did belong. And this job would help her do that.

After preparing for bed, and seeing it was too early to sleep, she headed for the library to find something to read. None of the titles on the spines seemed interesting and she didn't recognise most of the authors. Only a few were familiar, being as how they were classics. She started to randomly reach for one of the books.

"They are not for reading."

Esther spun to face Norman, who stood in the doorway. "They're books."

"You'll crease their spines and ruin the decor of the room."

She stared at Norman. Was he serious?

"The app store on your phone has plenty of books and a credit card has been linked to it. Purchase what you need to keep you entertained of an evening. Movies too."

"I can buy what I want from the app store?" She

said the words slowly, wanting to make sure he understood her. Since clearly she hadn't understood him. Who kept books as decorations? They were meant to be read.

"Yes." He paused a moment. "There's no reason for you to enter this room unless you need to leave items in here for Elvera."

Without commenting, she strode towards the doorway, unable to exit when Norman remained in place. She started to meet his gaze, lowering hers instead. She was meant to be changing the way she did things. Glaring at him and demanding he get out of the way, was not it. That was how she always ended up in a fight.

After a moment, Norman stepped out of the way. "I will collect you at nine tomorrow morning."

She glanced up at him. She had no idea what he was expecting her to say, but clearly he was waiting for something. "Thank you."

With a single nod, Norman strode towards the back of the house.

She stared after him. A month. No, four weeks. She could manage this for that long. Elvera had offered a grand a week since she'd be on call twenty-four seven. Surely she could last that long. It'd be enough to give her a start. And she wouldn't need to spend any of it since food and accommodation were covered.

Wandering towards her bedroom, she sighed. She had a feeling it would be yet one more job she wouldn't be able to mention due to the bad reference she'd end up with. There was such a long list of them. Entering the bedroom, she closed the door behind her, then dropped onto the bed, thinking about her first job. It had been a few hours every afternoon, after school, at a fish and chip shop.

A customer had come in fifteen minutes after she'd started work for the day, slamming the unwrapped parcel of fish and chips on the counter and complaining. It hadn't taken long before he was yelling and she started yelling back. The argument had ended with her throwing the food at him as her boss entered the shop. She'd lasted two and a half weeks. The worst part was it hadn't been the shortest amount of time she'd held a job.

She fell asleep reading on the phone, waking to the alarm she'd set before starting to read. Breakfast with Elvera was silent and afterwards, she checked over the calendar she'd found on the phone, noticing Elvera's appointments were all entered. Who had done this job before her? Had they become fed up with Elvera's disdainful looks and quit?

Not having anything more to do, Esther wandered out the back, pacing the patio. The immaculately kept backyard contained perfectly trimmed shrubs and tidy garden beds. It was almost a relief to go shopping with Norman. At least until she realised she'd have no say in what she would wear.

She tried to tell herself they were uniforms. But being told to try on a pair of designer jeans for casual wear had her gritting her teeth and hurrying towards the dressing room before she said something. None of the clothes were comfortable or designed for lying about in. It was going to be a really long four weeks.

Coming out of the dressing room, Esther checked the time on the phone. "Can we stop for lunch?"

"When we are finished." Norman took the jeans from her. "Did they fit?"

"Yes, but–"

"Good." He strode to the counter.

Chapter Three

Sighing, Esther followed Norman at a slower pace. Four weeks. Surely she could last four weeks. The job she'd lasted for the least amount of time came to mind. Although she shouldn't have been surprised she'd been fired before the first day had ended. Punching the boss was never a good idea. He'd been a complete arsehole and more than deserved it. At the time she'd been amazed she'd managed to ignore his belittling comments for three hours.

The shopping was completed half an hour later. Before Esther could suggest food again, a message came through on her phone from Elvera. It was an address and orders to collect a necklace. The front door would be left unlocked and the necklace was in the back bedroom on the left of the house.

Norman also received a message. He looked up

from his phone. "I'll drop you at the address and you can catch a taxi back."

She wanted to argue. Instead, she lowered her gaze. "Thank you." What else could she say? That she wanted lunch first? The drive to the location was silent and she stared out the window as they turned onto a street with numerous old trees creating shadowy areas along the footpath. The houses were quiet and the road empty.

Norman pulled up in front of a sprawling timber house, most of it hidden by three large trees with widespread branches. "I'll leave the clothes in the laundry for the cleaner to sort when she arrives tomorrow. She comes every Wednesday and Friday. If your room doesn't need cleaning, close the door."

When he continued to look expectantly at her, she struggled to think of what to say. "Thank you." She supposed the words were enough since he nodded. Relieved, she got out of the car and headed for the gate. Opening it, she strode towards the house. It was old, but well maintained. Not the sort of house she'd expect a friend of Elvera's to live in. Although she supposed they weren't necessarily a friend.

A glance over her shoulder showed that Norman had driven away. Movement at a window in the house across the street caught her attention. A shiver ran down her spine. Was someone watching her? She took a step towards the street, reminding herself she was a different person. The old her might have strode over there to demand what they were looking at, but not these days. She wasn't angry at the world and everything that had happened. The words seemed hollow. She mentally repeated them as she faced the house. They sounded no more convincing.

Checking the door, she found it unlocked. "Anyone home?" There was no answer. She took a step inside. "Hello?" Still no answer. She closed the door behind her, moving further into the dimly lit interior. It felt odd entering someone's house when they weren't home.

She slowly made her way towards the back of the house, looking for a bedroom on the left side. It didn't take long to find it. She remained in the doorway of the bedroom. The place seemed lifeless. There was a single bed with a plain bedspread against the far wall and a chest of drawers beside the bed, a necklace resting on it. Assuming it was the object Elvera had sent her to fetch, she hurried across the room and picked it up, dropping it inside her handbag. Before she could leave the room, two large males entered, stopping just inside the doorway.

For a moment she thought they were human. Then

she noticed unnaturally long claws, strange looking eyes and rows of pointed teeth crowding the mouth of the creature on the left when he grinned at her. She took a step back, running into the chest of drawers. "What are you?" The words were soft and for a moment she thought they couldn't possibly have heard her. She wasn't about to repeat herself. She needed to escape. All the horror movies she'd watched over the years came to mind. They couldn't be demons. Someone had to be playing a trick on her. Was this Elvera's sick idea of a joke?

The demon on the right stalked towards her. "What am I? I'm a really bad day for you." He stopped in front of her, grinning.

The scent of bushfire smoke washed over her. A shudder ran through her, old memories freezing her in place. Screams echoed in the recesses of her mind, ones that had haunted her dreams for years.

He grabbed hold of her wrist, drawing her closer. "Like a rabbit spotted by prey. No thoughts of running, human?"

She stared into his eyes, a flicker of flames in them. Memories swamped her. The crackle of flames, the searing heat, screams, sirens and the red glow in the night. "Please." She didn't know if she pleaded with him or the memories.

His claws tightened around her wrist, drawing blood. Raising her arm, he brought her wrist to his nose and breathed in deeply. "So sweet."

"If you get some of her blood, I should too," the one near the door said.

This couldn't be happening. None of it could be real. Had she tripped over something and hit her head, knocking herself out? "What are you?" Again her words were soft and uncertain. Did she really want an answer?

The creature near the door laughed. "She's not very bright."

The one in front of Esther also laughed, looking over his shoulder at his companion. "That's probably the best, for all involved. Easier in the long run." He faced Esther, leaning in close. "A demon. All your nightmares made real."

"You can't be real."

He laughed again. "You're about to find out exactly how real." He lowered his head, licking the blood from her skin.

Pain shot through her and she screamed, the sound echoing around her, echoed by the ones in her memories.

The demon by the door laughed, coming further into the room. "Scream all you want. There's no one to hear you except us. And your cries are music to our ears."

She fell silent at his words, the pain beginning to ebb. "Please." She met the gaze of the demon who held her. She saw no sympathy, only excitement. "Let me-" She broke off as three people burst into the bedroom, spreading out as they entered.

There was one female and two males and they all held swords. One of the males had a second sword sheathed at his side. He was young and dressed in black, his dark hair tied back in a ponytail at the nape of his neck. The female had blue eyes and light brown hair, while the other male had dark blond hair, piercing blue eyes and angular cheekbones. They all appeared to be around her age.

The demons faced the doorway, the first demon getting a better grip on Esther while the second one formed a sword from the air. "No one said the day would be so interesting. Four humans to play with."

"I don't think the day's going to be much fun for you." The young man with the ponytail drew his second sword and raced towards the demon who held Esther.

The demon pushed Esther from him and she stumbled against the chest of drawers, falling against them. When she regained her balance, demons and humans fought in the room, the sounds of swords clashing breaking the earlier silence. Esther slowly shook her head. This couldn't be happening. Had she spent all those years being angry and doing nothing with her life only to lose it when she'd finally decided it was time to change? It shouldn't surprise her if this was how it ended. With the stench of smoke. The same scent as when she'd cheated death.

A burst of light brought her back to the room, dragging her from old memories. She shielded her eyes, realising it had been a demon disappearing. She looked around the room. The other demon was gone too. Only the three armed humans were left. She retreated, the corner of the room preventing her from going further.

The young man with the ponytail sheathed his swords, taking a couple of steps towards Esther. "Are you okay?"

For once her first instinct wasn't to reply angrily or sarcastically. She looked at each of them, nodding then shaking her head. She had no idea how she was. "How–" She tried again when words failed her. "I've never–" What was she doing standing here? Just because these three had taken out the demons, that didn't mean she was safe.

The young man with the ponytail stepped a little closer. "You're safe now."

For a moment she thought she'd spoken the words aloud. But that would have made as much sense as everything else. Her gaze was drawn to her wrist and the deep scratch the demon had left behind. She fumbled in her handbag and drew out a tissue, pressing it against the scratch. "How can any of this be real?" She looked from the three standing in front of her to her wrist, occasionally glancing around the room as she assessed her options of escape.

"Why were they after you?" the other young man asked.

"I'm nobody." Esther drew back the tissue. "Nobody." Blood welled up along the scratch and she pressed the tissue against it again. Her gaze met the young woman's. "Why are you here? Why did you help me?" She had other questions. What felt like a million questions. But those ones seemed the most important. Why had they helped her and how had they known she was in danger? Was this a setup?

The young woman slowly smiled. "We're hunters. This is our job. It's what we do."

Esther was about to ask what a hunter was when the young man with the ponytail closed the distance between them.

He put his arm around her shoulders. "Let me take you home." He glanced at the second young man.

"We'll take care of things here."

Esther didn't argue when he ushered her out of the house and into the daylight. She took in deep breaths, the scent of smoke gone from the air. It was only left in her memories, ready to haunt her dreams. She pulled away from his arm. "Who are you?"

"Malachi." He grinned at her. "Malachi Hunter."

Her gaze narrowed. "Is this some kind of sick joke?"

"Absolutely not." He held out a hand. "Let me take you home."

"You want me to tell you where I live."

He laughed softly. "I can see how that might worry you. But I'm no danger to you. My family protects people from demons. We don't hurt them."

She caught a glimpse of a cross on a leather cord at his neck. "You're religious."

He lifted the cross. "That bothers you for some reason?"

It not only made her think of the disappointed looks from her last foster family, but also of Elvera. She couldn't lose this job. "I have to go." She headed for the gate she'd left open.

Malachi caught up with her. "Let me give you a lift

somewhere. It doesn't have to be to your home. Just somewhere you'll be safe."

She glanced at her wrist, the blood dry on her skin. "I have to return to work." That sounded better than saying she lived at her work. She came to an abrupt stop when she saw the sportscar out the front. "Is that yours?"

Malachi chuckled. "It's Luca's. Should I ask him to give you a lift home?"

She shook her head, starting down the street. "I don't need a lift." She just wanted to put this day behind her. Forget about it like that other day. Hopefully, she'd be more successful in forgetting this day.

"Is your work far from here?"

She had no idea. Glancing at him, her gaze was drawn to his swords. She stopped and faced him. "You're not going to wander the streets with them, are you?" She gestured towards the weapons. The last thing she needed was being picked up by the cops the day after she arrived in a new place. Already her new start was looking terrible.

Malachi grinned at her. "I thought you'd disappear if I took the time to leave them in my vehicle." He glanced back at the house they'd come from. "What were you doing there anyway? I assume you don't live there since you didn't yell at us to get out of your house. People tend to have that response, even after being saved from demons."

She supposed it wouldn't hurt to tell him. "My boss sent me there to pick up something."

"Did your boss know there were demons wandering around the place?"

She opened her mouth several times before she was able to answer. "Why would you think that? Most people don't believe demons exist. And what reason would she have to send me to where there are demons?"

"You turned up late to work one too many times?"

Her hands curled into fists and she felt like striking out at him. She knew it wasn't him she was angry at. He was just conveniently in front of her. She slowly let out her breath, trying to remain calm. Hitting the person who'd saved her from demons probably wasn't the way to thank them for their efforts. "It's my first day."

Malachi chuckled. "Talk about worst first day. It might be time to start searching for a new job."

"I need this one."

He slipped his arm around her shoulders. "I'll give you a lift back to work and my number in case your second day on the job is as bad as the first."

She pulled away from him again. "I don't need a lift."

"Humour me."

"Why?"

He stared at her a moment before he spoke. "To make sure you weren't the target and it was only a case of being in the wrong place at the wrong time."

Chapter Four

Fear washed over Esther and screams echoed in her mind along with the crackle of flames. "I have a tendency to be in the wrong place at the wrong time." She couldn't keep the bitterness from her words. She wasn't meant to have been at home that night. Had fought with her best friend earlier that day and refused to have a sleepover at her place. It had changed everything. Everyone's plans had been changed.

"Then let me give you a lift to work." He slipped his arm around her shoulders again, guiding her to his vehicle. "You never told me your name."

She contemplated not telling him. "Esther."

"A queen. I should have known." He lowered his arm as they reached his vehicle, opening the door.

"Queen?"

He gestured towards the front passenger seat,

holding the door open. "In the bible. She was a queen." He looked her up and down. "You have the bearing of one."

She wanted to protest his compliment. Did queens tend to get into fistfights? Make sarcastic comments and end up in more trouble than they knew what to do with? She seriously doubted it. "How will you tell if I'm the target?"

"I can sense demons when they're in an area."

She sat down hard. "You can…" She couldn't say the words. Didn't want to think them. Why did life always do this to her?

"Hop in properly and I'll give you a lift to work. Then I'll pick you up once you're finished for the day and see if where you live is safe."

She did as he said, her mind whirling with everything. Demons! How could they be real? She thought of the half a glass of wine she'd drunk last night. Maybe this was all an alcohol fuelled nightmare. She'd never been much of a drinker. And this was obviously the reason why. It gave her weird, life like nightmares.

Malachi closed the door and walked around to the other side of the vehicle. Once he was seated, he looked over at her. "What is the address?"

She slowly shook her head. "This can't be happening." She reached for the door handle.

Malachi leaned across and rested his hand on hers. "Wait. Don't run off."

She shrank back against the seat. Would he stop her from leaving? She should never have entered his vehicle. She obviously wasn't thinking clearly.

Malachi let her go, shifting back in his seat. "I won't stop you from leaving. Just open the glove box and take the business card with you. It's for Father Joe. You can call him and leave a message for me if you need help."

She opened the door before she opened the glove box, placing one foot on the edge of the gutter first. Amongst the various items was a sheathed dagger, several business cards and a cross on a leather cord. Eyeing the dagger, she took one of the business cards.

"Take the cross too," Malachi said. "It will help against demons."

She wanted to protest that demons weren't real, but her hand closed over the cross and she shoved it in her handbag along with the business card. She was half out of the vehicle before she looked back at him. "Thank you." Closing the door, she hurried down the street. She fought against the ridiculous urge to burst into tears. But they wouldn't help.

Taking her phone from her handbag, she put in Elvera's address, checking to see how far away it was as she tried to think of the last time she'd cried. Not since her second foster home. She'd listened at the door as her foster mum had spoken softly to her caseworker, asking that they find another home for her even though she'd done nothing wrong. It had taken several minutes for the truth to come out. 'It's the tears. There's so much sorrow and anguish in them that I can't bear to listen. She's breaking my heart and I can't do anything to help her. You have to find somewhere else for her to live.'

Turning the corner, Esther glanced back towards where Malachi's vehicle had been parked. It was gone. Just like she'd been gone from her second foster home impossibly fast, the caseworker unable to change her foster mum's mind.

Glancing at her phone, she saw Elvera's place was only an eight-minute walk away. At least according to the map. It'd take longer for a taxi to arrive. Slipping the phone in her handbag, she headed in the direction the map had shown her, trying not to think about what had happened. There was no way she could mention any of this to Elvera. The woman would think her crazy and probably fire her on the spot.

When she did reach the house, she stared at the front door. How was she meant to get inside? No one had given her a key. She stepped closer, about to knock on the door when she heard voices on the other side of it.

"They should have contacted me by now, Norman. Go and see what happened," Elvera said sharply.

"It hasn't been that lo-"

Elvera interrupted Norman. "If I say it has been too long, then it has been too long."

Esther shrank back from the door. She could still hear the voices. They must be right on the other side.

"I'll check on them immediately," Norman said.

"Nothing better go wrong with this deal. It should be simpler than all the others. It would seem there's no information I need to learn," Elvera said.

"What if it's all lies?" Norman asked.

"I'll give it a week. That should be more than enough time to tell if any of it is lies." Elvera paused a moment. "Now go and check on them."

Esther hurried across the front of the house, heading for the side that didn't have the garage. Slipping around it, she pressed herself against the wall, trying to slow her breathing. What deal was Elvera in the process of arranging? And who did she think had lied?

Before she'd applied for the job, she'd looked up the company the email address was for and discovered it was a reputable one with various holdings. But what if they'd faked the email address or if someone had hacked into the company and had all the emails forwarded and-

She broke off the thought, trying to convince herself she was being ridiculous. The demons had unsettled her. This had to be a nightmare. She'd play it through and when she headed to bed again in the dream, she'd wake up and it'd be Tuesday. The real Tuesday. Not this fake one.

Taking a deep breath, she pushed away from the wall of the house and strode towards the front door. This time when she paused at it before knocking, there was silence on the other side. She knocked twice on the door and waited for an answer. Silence dragged out and she began to think no one would answer. It wasn't like the house was small. What if Elvera had been upstairs? Or out the back. She started to knock again.

The door swung open. Elvera looked her up and down. "Didn't you go shopping this morning?"

"Yes."

"Then where are the clothes that were purchased for you?"

Esther opened her mouth to argue the accusation. She closed it instead, taking the necklace out of her handbag. She held it out to Elvera.

The woman barely glanced at the necklace. "Did you collect it without a problem?"

"The afternoon didn't go exactly as I expected." She hurriedly spoke again when it looked like Elvera might speak. She didn't want to answer any questions. "Did you want me to put it somewhere for you?"

Elvera snatched the necklace from her. "Your hair is a mess. Did you make that appointment as I requested?"

She slowly breathed out before answering. "I'll do that now." She glanced past Elvera when she didn't step out of the way.

"I'll have Norman organise a key for you." Elvera looked Esther up and down once more. "See that you wear something appropriate to dinner this evening." She started to turn away, facing Esther again. "You may use the phone I gave you to call friends."

She started to thank Elvera, changing her mind at the last second. Was the woman testing what she'd told her yesterday? Was she the one suspected of lying? Or did Elvera think everyone a liar? "Thanks for the offer, but there's no one to ring."

Elvera inclined her head then headed towards the stairs.

Esther didn't step inside until Elvera was out of view. She closed the front door behind her. How was she going to cope with four weeks of this? She hadn't managed a single day without disaster. She started to head to her bedroom, remembering at the last second that her new clothes would need washing before tonight if she was expected to wear something appropriate to dinner. Appropriate according to Elvera.

Once again, Esther was nearly late to dinner. Not that it was her fault. Washing and drying clothes took time. As did ironing them. She'd also had to google how to use the fancy appliances she'd found in the laundry. So it was amazing she'd managed to arrive on time at all.

Elvera looked Esther up and down before indicating the chair she'd sat in the previous night. "A slight improvement. A trip to the salon will help."

Esther stared at the plate Norman placed in front of her, trying not to panic. She'd completely forgotten to make the appointment. She'd been too busy trying to get ready for the evening. She frantically tried to think of something to say before Elvera could ask her anything about the appointment. "Who cooks the meals? This looks as good as last night's."

Elvera pressed a finger to her lips. "No needless chatter at the table. That isn't why you're here." She turned to Norman with a smile. "Wine please, Norman. My favourite."

"Immediately." Norman strode towards the kitchen.

"You will enjoy this wine," Elvera said.

Esther had a mouthful of food rather than reply. After all, she wasn't here to chatter so arguing would probably be even more frowned upon. She had a sip of the wine when Norman poured it, the dark red liquid filling the glass almost to the brim. She wanted to protest that it was more than last night. Was she expected to have wine with every meal?

"Did I not tell you it was good?" Elvera had a sip of her wine.

"You did." Esther managed not to smile. Just because Elvera said something, that didn't make it true. "It would go nice with chocolate." Something to make the bitter drink more bearable. If anything, it was more bitter than the one last night. Couldn't the woman prefer a sweeter wine?

"I'll let Norman know you would like chocolate with your wine," Elvera said.

Once again she remained silent, congratulating herself on not answering back. That hadn't been what she'd said at all.

Norman entered the room, holding out a mobile phone. "You might wish to take this call."

"Can you not see I'm having dinner?" Elvera placed her cutlery down.

"It's regarding the earlier matter we discussed." Norman continued to hold the phone out.

Elvera slowly rose from the table. "I will take it in the library." She strode from the table, Norman following her.

Esther waited until they were out of sight before she grabbed the wine glass and hurried to the kitchen, tipping most of it down the sink. She was careful to pour it directly down the drain. Turning on the tap would have given away that she'd left the table. She was seated and eating again when Elvera returned.

Once seated, Elvera looked between their two plates. "You could not have waited for my return?"

Esther swallowed her mouthful. "Sorry."

Elvera held her gaze for a moment. "I expect this will not happen again."

"No, of course not." She lowered her gaze when Elvera continued to watch her. She tried not to give in to the anger that washed through her. For all her fancy ways, Elvera was a bully. How was she supposed to know not to eat? Besides, she was starving. Elvera hadn't given her a chance to eat lunch today.

Once she'd finished eating, Elvera remained at the table, sipping her wine.

Esther glanced at Elvera's glass several times, but the contents seemed to be going down too slowly. She didn't want to sit in this awkward silence a moment longer. "I'm tired. Do you mind if I get ready for bed now?" She looked up, meeting Elvera's gaze when the woman didn't answer.

Elvera examined her carefully. "I daresay you are." She nodded towards the almost empty wine glass in front of Esther. "Finish your wine, then off you go."

She had the last mouthful of wine, trying not to make a face at how bitter it was.

Elvera frowned. "You really are a barbarian at times." She made a shooing motion with her hand. "Off to bed. I'll see you at breakfast."

Anger kept her at the table another few seconds as she struggled to remain silent, her gaze focused on the glass she'd placed on the table. Eventually, she was able to bring herself to rise and speak without fear the anger would fill her words. "Goodnight."

Elvera inclined her head, saying nothing.

Chapter Five

Once in her room, Esther closed the door, leaning against it, her hands curled into fists. She wanted to smash something. Wanted to show Elvera what a barbarian was really like. It wasn't someone who downed the last of their wine in a single mouthful. She could hear the sound of fist meeting flesh echoing in her memories. The muscles in her arms tensed as she recalled fights. Both ones she'd lost and those she'd won.

She shouldn't let the woman get to her. Nor did she expect Elvera would fight her own battles. Norman would be called upon to do that. Just like he was called upon to pour the wine and take barbarians shopping. She closed her eyes, trying to forget the anger. Barbarian. It wasn't the first time she'd been called that. A teacher had that honour. He hadn't asked what she was fighting about. Just assumed she was to blame. The kid she'd hit had said her parents had deliberately died so they didn't have to put up with her. He'd never made another comment like that again. At least not to her face.

Breathing out slowly, Esther pushed away from the door. She hadn't completely been lying when she'd told Elvera she was tired. It had been just a little, but that little was slowly increasing. Maybe she should sleep. At least then this first disastrous day would be over and she'd only have another three weeks and six days to get through. It was starting to look like it'd be an eternity. Unless of course this day was a nightmare and she'd wake in the morning with four weeks still to get through.

Esther fell asleep the moment her head touched the pillow. She had no idea how long she slept before warm hands against her cheeks woke her. Darkness surrounded her and she struggled to make sense of what was happening. Warmth washed over her lips, the hands tightening on her face as she sank into sleep again.

She struggled to wake, finding herself staring into a mirror, running a finger across the skin beside her eyes. She stared into her eyes, the familiar hazel colour meeting her gaze. "I can work with this."

Her voice filled the silence of the bathroom and she smiled.

Everything faded and when she surfaced again, she was sitting in the lounge room, glaring at one of the demons from that afternoon. It was then that she realised she must be dreaming. It was the only logical explanation. "I don't want to hear your excuses or your demands." Her lips curved into a smile. "Or your failures."

"Then why did you tell me to meet you here?" the demon demanded.

"Tell me what happened."

"She's weak. Didn't fight us. If those hunters hadn't turned up, she probably would have fainted in fear," the demon said.

Esther struggled not to lose her grip on the dream. She wanted to argue with the demon. Other words came out instead. "How could you have let hunters know you were in the area?"

"We stayed outside like you said. Waited until she arrived before entering. We did everything you said."

Confusion washed over Esther. Everything she said? As if she'd wanted anything to do with demons. Again the words she spoke weren't the ones she wanted to say. "You will get rid of the hunters. I will have no one interfere in my business." She placed the wine glass on the coffee table and rose to her feet. "Do you understand?"

"Yes."

"Then when I have finished with my body, you may have the blood." She made a dismissive gesture and the demon nodded before hurrying away. Sitting down again, she picked up the glass of wine and had a sip. "It's past time."

The dream faded and Esther struggled to bring it back. This time, she stood at the foot of her bed, watching Elvera who lay on her side facing a pillow with a dent where a head had lain. She walked alongside the bed, lifting a lock of dark hair from Elvera's head. "You have outlived your usefulness." She let the strands fall.

Esther struggled to hold onto the dream. This time, instead of falling into another dream, she opened her eyes to stare at the empty stretch of bed beside her. She was awake. Frowning, she sat up. Or was she? She ran her hands over her arms, pinching herself. Yes, she was finally awake. She dropped back onto her pillow, trying to remember her disjointed dreams from the night before.

Her mind was seriously messed up right now. She had no idea what half of it meant. Although she could guess part of it was due to her helplessness when she'd faced the demons yesterday and her anger at Elvera. Probably all of it was due to those two things. Sitting up again, she spied a strand of dark hair in front of the smooth pillow on the bed beside her.

Had Elvera been in her room? Anger rushed through her. She didn't care how much Elvera was paying her, she wasn't about to put up with her coming into her bedroom. Striding across the room, she flung the door open, freezing when she saw a woman walking past.

The woman slowed, looking towards her and coming to a stop with a smile. "You must be Esther." She came forward, holding out her hand, her black hair drawn into a ponytail set high at the back of her head. "They've probably already told you I'm here Wednesday and Friday."

Esther nodded, shaking the woman's hand.

"Well, you leave your door open if you want me to clean your room and I change the sheets on a Friday."

"Okay." Her gaze was drawn to the woman's black hair and she felt like an idiot. Why would Elvera want to enter her room? The woman thought she was a barbarian. Before she had the chance to ask the cleaner what her name was, the woman strode away. Esther returned to her room, closing the door.

She had to stop jumping to conclusions. And getting angry. This was meant to be a new start.

The demons came to mind. Not much of a new start. She breathed out slowly, trying to calm herself. It didn't help. She doubted anything would. Pushing away from the door she leaned against, she grabbed her bag and tipped the contents onto the bed. Picking up the business card and cross she considered ringing and leaving a message for Malachi. But what if Elvera checked the phone to see what calls she made?

She needed her own phone. One that no one could check who she'd rung. And she didn't even know the number for the phone Elvera had given her. Putting everything back in her handbag, she started to put the cross in too. At the last moment, she put it on, leaving the leather cord loose so she'd be able to tuck the cross beneath her clothes.

It didn't take her long to get ready for the morning and join Elvera at the table. Breakfast was a silent affair and Esther sent frequent glances at Elvera, relieved when she could finally leave the table. She hadn't gone far when a text message came through with a list of errands Elvera wanted her to run and that there was a key in the drawing room for her. Before she left her bedroom, she made the appointment she'd forgotten to make yesterday. They couldn't fit her in until the end of the week.

While she was out doing errands she picked up a phone with some of the money Norman had given her, sighing heavily at how much she'd spent and would have to take out of her first pay. She sat on a seat in the food court of a shopping centre, staring at the business card, the phone in her hand. In the end, she sent a text to Father Joe rather than ring him, requesting that Malachi contact her. Then she put her phone on silent, not wanting to let Elvera know she had it. When she left in three weeks and six days, she didn't want the woman to have any way of contacting her.

She stared at the phone, but it didn't ring. It wasn't until she was on the way back to Elvera's place, taking a bus rather than catching a taxi like she'd been told, that her new phone rang. There was no number on the screen, only the word 'private'. "Hello?"

"It's Malachi. Father Joe said you wanted to talk to me."

She had no idea what to say. Calling him seemed foolish now she could hear him on the other end of the phone. "I'm sorry. I shouldn't have-"

"I take it you arrived home okay."

"Yeah."

"No more demon encounters?"

"Not unless you count dreams." She tried not to think about her strange dreams.

"Are you sure they were dreams?"

"They must have been. It was the demon you…" She hesitated, glancing at the woman several seats away and lowering her voice before she finished the sentence. "Killed."

"They aren't dead, Esther. It doesn't work like that. So are you sure it was a dream?"

She leaned back against the vinyl seat. What did he mean they weren't dead? "I saw you. Saw them."

"They were returned to hell. That doesn't mean they can't be summoned again."

The bus pulled up and she saw it was her stop. "I have to go." She gathered her shopping bags.

"Wait-"

"I shouldn't have called." She hung up on his protests, heading for the exit. As she stepped off the bus, a text message came through, the phone vibrating in her hand to notify her. She paused on the footpath. He'd sent his number with a message to call him any time. She stared at the words. It was all so crazy. Demons shouldn't exist.

Dropping her phone into her handbag, she strode down the street, headed for Elvera's house. From now on, she'd stay away from strange locations. She thought of her last foster parents and their numerous crosses around the house and the smaller ones they wore on necklaces. Was that why she'd never encountered demons in the time she'd lived with them? Was that all it took to keep demons away? She lightly touched the cross through the material of her top. If that was all, then she was never taking the cross off again.

Reaching the house, she dug the key out of her handbag and let herself inside, leaving the shopping bags in the library on one of the armchairs. The rest of the day was spent pacing her room, in between reading and watching movies on the phone from Elvera. Not that the evening was any better as she tried to find a way to avoid drinking the bitter wine Elvera had Norman serve with dinner.

It was impossible and she found herself drinking the last drop in her glass, declining the chocolate Elvera said was in the fridge. She rose to her feet. "I might head to bed. I'm really tired." Obviously doing nothing all day was exhausting. She needed to find a hobby or something. She couldn't spend the next three weeks and six days aimlessly pacing the bedroom.

Elvera inclined her head. "Sleep well." She smiled

before taking a sip of her glass of wine that was almost empty.

"Ah… thanks." She took a step back, unsettled by Elvera's smile. "I'll see you in the morning." Exhaustion tugged at her, making it difficult to keep her eyes open.

"I'll see you at breakfast." Elvera remained seated.

Esther hurried to her room, readying herself for bed in record time, barely remembering dropping onto the bed and falling asleep. A sharp pain woke her in the night, a burning sensation against her chest and she struggled to make sense of what was happening. A shadow moved away from her with a sharp, indrawn breath. She sank back into sleep, waking early in the morning with a headache.

She lay where she was, staring at the ceiling in the dim light of morning. The night came back to her and she brushed her fingers across where she'd felt the pain. It was uncomfortable. Rising, she went to the ensuite and checked in the mirror. Shifting the cross to the side, she found a red mark on her skin, like something had burned her. She frowned. Had an insect bitten her in the night? Returning to her bed, she checked for spiders and stinging type creatures. There were none. Her fingers brushed across the spot on her chest again.

Returning to the bathroom, she examined the mark once more. Frowning, she moved closer to the mirror, wishing the vanity wasn't in the way. It could almost be the shape of a cross. That was weird. Was she allergic to the metals the cross was made from? Maybe it wasn't gold like she'd first thought.

Returning to her room, she rummaged in her handbag for her phone, adding Malachi's number to her contacts before sending him a message to ask him what the cross was made of. He replied almost instantly. She slowly shook her head. That couldn't be possible. Surely it wasn't only made of gold.

Are you sure? She stared at the phone, waiting for a reply.

What happened?

She had no idea what to tell him. *Nothing. I guess it was an insect or something.*

Can I see you?

I'm fine. I told you. It was nothing.

The cross has been blessed and dipped in holy water.

She read the words over three times. They didn't change. *What does that mean?*

The phone vibrated. Malachi's name was displayed on the screen.

She declined the call, not wanting to talk to him.

What exactly could she tell him? Nothing. Because nothing had happened.

Talk to me, Esther. What happened?

Everything is fine. I already told you. Nothing happened. She returned the phone to her handbag, not wanting to know if he messaged her again.

Chapter Six

Esther paced the room then tried to read something. But she was too restless to settle and her fingers kept brushing across the mark on her chest as she tried not to think about it or anything else for that matter. It was almost a relief to join Elvera at the table for breakfast.

Elvera gestured towards a fine gold chain with a small, red stone in a decorative setting hanging from it. "The leather cord of your necklace does not suit your clothes. It's tacky. You can wear this old necklace of mine."

"Thank you." She sat at the table and began to eat her breakfast.

Elvera continued to watch her. "Did you hear what I said?"

Looking up from her plate, Esther nodded, hurriedly swallowing her mouthful. "Yes."

"Then why have you not removed that tacky necklace?"

"I was going to change it after breakfast."

Elvera slid the necklace closer to her. "You would force me to sit through a meal with you wearing that tasteless bit of leather around your throat?"

Esther met Elvera's gaze, about to demand if she was allowed to choose any of the things she wore. Before she could do something so stupid, she lowered her gaze and breathed out slowly. "Sorry." She slipped the leather cord over her head and let the necklace drop onto her lap.

"Didn't you say you weren't religious?" Elvera gestured towards Esther.

Rather than answer, Esther picked the necklace up off the table and fumbled with the catch. She could manage this. Three weeks and five days.

"How hard can it be to undo the clasp?" Rising to her feet, Elvera took the necklace from Esther and undid the clasp. "Hold your hair out of the way." She stepped around Esther to stand behind her.

Esther wanted to get out of the chair. She didn't like having Elvera stand over her where she couldn't see what she was doing. She tried to shake the unnerving feeling, but it persisted. Lifting her hair off the nape of her neck, she held herself still.

Elvera leaned close, brushing against Esther as she slipped the necklace around her neck. She tugged it close to Esther's skin as she did up the clasp.

Esther started to raise her hand, about to tug the necklace away from her throat, when Elvera released it and it slipped down so that the pendant rested against her top. Looking down at it, she also saw the cross lying on her lap. She would have preferred to wear it rather than the fancy necklace Elvera had put around her throat. She slowly let out her breath. "Thank you." The words were soft, spoken reluctantly. She was getting sick of thanking people who didn't deserve to be thanked.

Elvera returned to her seat. She stared at Esther before picking up her cutlery. "That is far more suitable."

Not wanting to talk about the necklace any further, Esther tried to think of a way to change the topic. Nothing came to mind. "Is there anything you need me to do for you today?"

Elvera placed her cutlery beside her plate again. "If I need you to do something for me, I will send you a message. I do not wish to be pestered in this way."

Esther lowered her gaze again. "Sorry." She continued eating her food, remaining silent rather than argue the comment. The moment she'd finished eating, she rose to her feet, catching the cross before it fell. She glanced at Elvera. When the woman said nothing, only continued to eat, Esther hurried away from the table.

Returning to her room, she dropped onto the bed, her gaze drawn to the cross she held. She was tempted to take off the necklace Elvera had put on her and slip the leather cord over her head.

The cross made her think of Malachi. She could barely recall what the two with him had looked like, but she could easily bring him to mind. What sort of person hunted demons? Who put themselves in danger to save other people? It reminded her of the firefighters. She couldn't recall a single one of their faces, only the flames from that night so long ago. Although sometimes it felt like it was only last week, the stench of smoke filling her lungs, causing her to cough and her eyes to water.

She surged to her feet. Sitting around doing nothing was going to send her crazy. It'd give her time to think about things she'd rather put behind her. So much for a new start. Was that possible? She slipped the cross into her handbag then checked her phone for messages from Elvera. There were none. There was a message from Malachi.

Give me a street name. I won't need a number. Just a

name. I'll be able to tell you if any demons are on that street just by walking down it.

She drew in a shaky breath. There were no demons on this street. She didn't need him to walk along it to tell her that. The demons had been nothing to do with her. She'd been in the wrong place at the wrong time. Shoving the phones inside her handbag, she grabbed it and headed for the front door. She had to get out of here for awhile. Go for a walk or something.

Elvera came out of the library before Esther reached the front door. "Are you going somewhere?"

"I thought I'd take a walk. Get some exercise."

Elvera looked her up and down. "A very good point. You could do with some exercise. I'll have Norman arrange for you to visit the fitness centre I use and have the personal trainer set up a program for you." She strode towards the stairs.

Esther remained where she was, mouth slightly open as she stared sightlessly at the door. She slowly turned, catching sight of Elvera as she disappeared up the stairs. Her hands tightened into fists and she breathed out slowly. It didn't help. Her jaw tightened as she returned to her bedroom. Had that been Elvera's way of not only insulting her, but telling her not to go for a walk? She didn't know. Closing her bedroom door softly behind her, she leaned against it. Three weeks and five days. Surely she could manage to last here that long. By being extra frugal she could make that amount of money last quite awhile. It'd give her plenty of time to find something better.

Crossing the room, she dropped onto the bed, taking her phone out of the handbag. She stared at the message from Malachi, putting her phone away with a sigh. He wasn't the type of person she should get to know. Ordinary people with ordinary lives died. How greater a chance was death for people who went out seeking danger?

Trying to take her mind off her thoughts, she took out the phone from Elvera and struggled to focus on the book she'd started reading yesterday. The day passed slowly. The only things she needed to do was send two messages to Elvera at different times during the day to remind her of appointments. It hardly seemed worth the money she was earning. Although being stuck at the house and unable to go anywhere was extremely boring.

As seven o'clock approached, Esther reluctantly dressed for dinner. She made sure the pendant from Elvera remained displayed against the fabric of her dress. Satisfied with how she looked, she left the bedroom, arriving at the table before Elvera. She wasn't sure if she should remain standing or sit down.

Elvera joined her within minutes. "I was beginning to think you weren't capable of dressing yourself properly. It's nice to see I was wrong."

Esther somehow managed not to say anything. It was close. She sat at the table, like Elvera did, and kept her gaze on the table in front of her rather than glare at Elvera. Once more, she reminded herself of how many days she had to get through. She was beginning to think she'd be lucky to last a week. Not because she'd quit, but because she'd be fired.

Norman placed a plate of food in front of each of them and filled their wine glasses. When Elvera thanked him, he nodded and headed outside.

Esther tried not to glare at the glass of wine. She was sick of the bitter drink Elvera expected her to have each night. And she was sick of having to hold her tongue rather than speak the words that came to mind. Slowly letting out her breath, she began to eat, taking a sip of wine. It was as bitter as the previous ones.

Partway through the meal, Norman returned, holding a mobile phone. "Nethod wishes to speak to you."

"How many times must I tell you I do not wish to be disturbed while having a meal?" Elvera demanded.

Norman held out the phone. "I thought you'd want to take this call. That you'd want to hear what he has to say."

Elvera held his gaze for a moment before she slowly rose to her feet and strode from the room.

Norman followed.

Esther looked from the wine glass to the direction the two of them had disappeared in. It didn't take long to come to a decision. Grabbing the wine glass, she hurried to the sink and tipped most of it down the drain. She was back at the table, eating her meal before they returned. It was an effort to keep her expression neutral. She glanced up at Elvera. "Is everything okay?"

Elvera picked up the cutlery. "My affairs are none of your concern."

The frosty tone sent a shiver down Esther's spine. She kept her gaze on the food in front of her. "Sorry."

"I see you are still incapable of using your manners." Elvera looked pointedly at the food in front of Esther.

Protests automatically rose. Esther held them back. "Sorry. I forgot." It was more accurate that she'd been worried about being caught getting rid of most of the wine to remember Elvera expected her to wait until she returned before continuing the meal.

"I expect you to pay proper attention to what I say, in future."

Esther nodded, waiting until Elvera ate before she continued to eat too. The rest of the meal was silent and Esther was relieved to finish eating so she could leave the table. She started to rise.

Elvera gestured towards the bit of wine left in the bottom of the glass. "You do not plan to waste that, do you?"

Esther sat back on the seat. "No. Of course not." She downed the rest of the wine before rising again. "I'll see you at breakfast. I might have an early night. I'm tired." Tired of remaining silent to be more accurate.

Elvera inclined her head, not commenting.

Esther hurried to her room. After getting ready for bed, she checked both the phones. There was another message from Malachi, asking if she was okay. Smiling, she replied. *I've had worse days.*

Can I help?

She considered answering, but decided not to encourage him. Did she really want to be friends with someone who hunted demons? Who put their life at risk all the time. She started to place the phone on top of the bedside drawers next to the phone from Elvera. At the last second, she tucked it in under the mattress. Removing the pendant Elvera had put around her neck, she dropped it on the bedside drawers. Staring at it lying in a pool made her think of the cross from Malachi. Again she thought of the mark left behind on her chest. What had caused it?

Wanting to figure it out, she put the cross back on in an effort to recreate the previous night. Lying down, planning to read, she struggled to remain awake, surprisingly tired. Turning off the bedside lamp, she closed her eyes and sank into a deep sleep.

Again Esther was woken by a sharp pain followed by a burning sensation against her chest. Her mind felt muddled and confused as she struggled to make sense of her surroundings. A shadowy figure loomed over her, drawing back with a hiss of sound. She watched the figure shift away, moving towards the door. Lethargy tugged at her and she struggled against it, trying to sit up so she could get a better look at what was going on around her. Her eyes struggled to remain open and she couldn't focus on the dark surroundings. The soft sound of the bedroom door closing had her dropping back onto the bed and sinking into sleep.

Early morning light woke her and she lay in bed,

thinking about the previous night. It felt like a dream. One of those sorts of dreams it was impossible to wake from. The type that never made sense. Slipping out of bed, she rubbed her temples. Regularly waking with a headache was becoming annoying.

While getting ready for the morning, she noticed another mark on her chest, similar to the previous one. Running her fingers across it, she frowned. She was no closer to figuring out what was going on than the previous day. Sighing, she finished getting ready, swapping necklaces before sprawling across the bed and returning to the book she was reading.

Becoming engrossed in the story, she was nearly late for breakfast, reaching the table a couple of minutes after seven. "Sorry." She slipped into place.

"Did you throw out that tacky cross you were wearing yesterday?" Elvera asked.

She glanced up at the woman, trying to judge her mood by her expression. It didn't help. Nor had the tone of her voice. "No."

"I will not have it in my house. I do not approve of what it stands for." Elvera rose from her seat. "Collect it immediately and throw it in the rubbish bin outside by the garage."

"That is ridiculous."

Elvera didn't speak straight away. "I beg your pardon."

Chapter Seven

Esther lowered her gaze, fear and anger colliding in her at the tone Elvera used. "I'll get it." She hurried to the bedroom, frantically trying to think of a way to avoid throwing it out. Closing the bedroom door behind her she looked at the dress she wore. The garment didn't contain a single pocket.

It was a medium weight material with long sleeves that had fancy cuffs. The dress reached her knees, hugging her body, leaving no hiding places. Her gaze was again drawn to the sleeves. She rolled them up several times and tested tucking the cross inside the fold. A smile slowly formed. That should work.

Hurrying outside, and through the back door, she nearly groaned when Elvera followed. Picking up her pace, she reached the bin well before Elvera and opened the lid to let it bang open against the plastic side. After tucking the cross and leather cord into the fold of the sleeve, she closed the lid of the bin and turned to face Elvera as she reached her side.

"What are you doing to your dress? Roll your sleeves down. That looks terrible," Elvera ordered.

"I didn't realise the day would warm up so much." She hurried back to the house.

Elvera walked beside her. "Roll your sleeves down and change your clothes after breakfast. Surely you don't expect me to sit at the table with you looking like that."

"You're right. I should change out of the dress." She picked up her pace. "Then you won't be sitting at the table with me stinking of sweat." Stepping inside, she hurried towards her room.

"I have not finished talking to you, Esther."

Ignoring Elvera, she stepped into the room, closing the door. She barely had time to slip the cross under the mattress of the bed before there was a knock at the door. Opening it, she met Elvera's angry gaze. The woman did not look at all impressed.

"Roll down your sleeves and return to the table." Elvera's words were both soft and sharp.

"I didn't think you'd want-"

Elvera interrupted her. "Return to the table and fix your sleeves."

Nodding, Esther did as she was told. The rest of the

meal was silent and uncomfortable. She was relieved to escape to her room. She'd no sooner closed the door, when she heard her phone notifying her of a message. It was a list of errands Elvera expected her to run.

She was kept busy the rest of the day travelling all across the city doing tedious tasks, as well as needing to go to the salon appointment. They were as lacking in compliments as Elvera and she couldn't help wondering if they spoke to her boss the same way. She impatiently sat through a manicure and pedicure and had her hair trimmed and a treatment put through it. In the end, she felt like saying she could see no difference when they told her she looked much better. Instead, she lied and agreed with them in case they reported her comment to Elvera. She barely had enough time to shower and dress for dinner. This time it was a knock at the front door that interrupted their meal.

The moment Elvera went to answer it, Esther took the chance to tip most of her wine down the sink. She was barely seated before Elvera headed back to the table. She kept her gaze on her plate as she tried to keep her breathing slow and steady. That had been too close. She had a sip of the wine to give herself something to do while she waited for Elvera to sit at the table. What would Elvera have said if she'd caught her in the act? She dreaded to think.

Like the previous nights, she used the excuse that she was tired to leave the table as soon as she'd finished. Not that it was that far from the truth. She was tired. Slipping into bed, she wondered if she should make a doctor's appointment to have her iron levels checked or something. She didn't normally sleep as much as she'd been sleeping lately.

She fell instantly asleep, dreaming of hands against her cheeks, the soft breath of someone facing her brushing across her lips. The dream changed. This time she answered the door, staring at one of the demons who had tried to kill her the other day.

"You're wasting your time, Nethod. I told you earlier that it has nothing to do with me if your companion was returned to hell."

"I've been thinking about that. You owe me. If you hadn't sent us to test her we wouldn't have come to the attention of the hunters. You need to organise someone to summon Torrnon," Nethod stated.

"Do you know who I am?" The tone of her own voice startled Esther. She'd never before used such a haughty one.

Nethod chuckled. "I know who you are. We all do.

And being stuck in a human body has its limitations. You think none of us knows that?"

"My power outweighs those limitations. I have walked this earth for centuries. And each year my power grows." She met Nethod's gaze. "You had best remember that. In my original body, I would have been forced to only walk the earth at night."

"But you don't have your original body." Nethod pointed a finger at her. "You're stuck choosing another and I have tasted the blood of this one."

When Esther would have recoiled from Nethod's venomous words, her body had other ideas and she grabbed the front of Nethod's shirt, bringing his face close to hers. "There are ways to permanently eliminate demons and I know every single one of them." She smiled at him. "Do I need to explain any of them to you?"

Nethod struggled to pull away from her grip. "How am I meant to get my brother back?"

She let him go and he stumbled from her. "How is that my problem?"

"Because you owe me."

"No. I don't. Stop ringing me and stop visiting the house. Next time there will be no warning. I'll make sure you never bother me again." She closed the door, striding towards her bedroom.

Picking up the phone, she checked through the calls and messages sent and received. Next, she rummaged through her handbag. She struggled to hold onto the dream, trying to figure out what she was looking for. Yet it was as if her body was a separate entity and her mind had a portion that she couldn't access. The sensation was strange and jarred her from the dream.

The next dream, she recalled, she was in an ornate bathroom, water running in the tub, the colour scheme similar to Elvera's house. A glass of wine was sitting on the edge of the tub and candles were lit around the room. She looked into a mirror above a spacious vanity, her fingers lightly running across her face. "Much better." She stared into her hazel eyes. "Coloured contacts can deal with that problem."

Shock arrowed through her. The dream was dragged from her grasp. She never used contacts. The thought of putting them in her eyes made her shudder. As much as she tried to wake, it was impossible. She wanted to drag herself out of sleep and assure herself that everything was normal.

In the next dream she pricked her finger, letting several drops of blood drip into a glass. She left it on the coffee table in the lounge room before returning to her room. The light was off, but she didn't bother to put it on. Closing the door, she lay on the bed, rolling onto her side. There was a shadowy figure in the bed and she placed her hands on the figure's cheeks, breathing softly against their lips. Her body relaxed and she felt herself separate into millions of pieces, nothing making sense. Darkness crashed in on her.

Fear followed the darkness and she struggled to wake, hearing the sound of her bedroom door softly closing behind her. She lay awake in the dark, rolling onto her back as she ran her hands over her body. She both felt like herself and felt like someone else. What was going on? Sitting up, she reached for the bedside lamp, drawing her hand back before she could touch it. Instead, she took her phone from beneath the mattress and used the muted light to shine it around the bedroom. Everything looked the same as it had been when she'd gone to sleep.

It didn't make her feel any better. Wanting to feel less alone, she sent a text to Malachi. *Can demons be permanently killed?* She was surprised an answer came through within minutes.

What happened?

Strange dreams. Can they?

There are a handful of ways. Most of them involve another demon.

She lay back against the bed, not sure if she wanted to check on the rest of the things she'd said in her dream. She rubbed at her temples, realising she had a mild headache. Hopefully it would go as quickly as the ones from the previous days had gone. When her phone notified her of an incoming message, she checked what it was.

Did something happen?

She had no idea what to tell Malachi. She sent him the name of the street, asking him if he'd walk along it tomorrow.

Did you want me to come now?

No. It's too early in the morning.

I am awake.

She smiled at his reply. *After breakfast will be fine. I'm going back to sleep.*

Goodnight.

Still smiling, she tucked the phone beneath the mattress. She felt less unnerved after chatting to him. Less alone. Rolling onto her side, she closed her eyes. He'd walk the street tomorrow morning and tell her there was nothing for her to worry about. That there were no demons in the house. She drifted off to sleep, still smiling.

Breakfast was the usual chore and she ate as quickly as possible without risking being called a barbarian.

She reminded herself several times that there were only three weeks and three days left. It was going to feel like an eternity. Escaping to her room, she took the phone out from under the mattress.

There were three missed calls and a text message. After seeing the calls were from Malachi, she checked the message. She had to read it over several times.

There is a demon in the house. Get out. If I don't hear from you within ten minutes, I'm coming in after you.

She checked the time. It had been eight minutes. She quickly sent a text. *I'm okay. Don't come in.* When the phone rang, she declined the call, worried Elvera or Norman might hear her talking.

Answer me.

I can't. Someone might hear me talking to you.

Then come outside.

A message came through on her phone from Elvera. She smiled. Elvera needed her to cancel the morning's appointments as she now had other plans for the day. It didn't take her long to cancel the appointments and let Elvera know it had been done. Malachi sent two messages during the time it took her to deal with the task.

Are you okay? Has something happened?

Answer me, Esther. I'm worried about you.

She smiled at the second message. *You don't know me. Why should you be worried?*

The demon has left.

Changing into a pair of old jeans and a t-shirt, she slipped a phone in each front pocket. Searching all of downstairs, she found the place was empty. She stood at the foot of the stairs, looking up them. Was Elvera up there? When her phone notified her of another message, she checked. It was Malachi again.

Are you still okay? Should I come in?

Who left in the car?

A man and a woman.

Smiling, she strode towards the front door and opened it. Before she could send him a text to ask him where he was, he stepped out from behind the wide trunk of an old tree that was on the other side of the road and strode towards her. She waited until he reached her before she spoke. "How can you tell if there are demons in a house?"

He glanced at his left wrist and the reddish black lines that wrapped around it four times. "Demon mark."

"How do you get one of them?"

"By facing demons and sending them back to hell."

"Not by killing them?"

"That would do it too, but that isn't what we do.

It's nearly impossible unless you're a demon." He gestured to the house behind her. "Can I come in?"

Her gaze was drawn to where his swords had hung last time she'd seen him. "Where are your weapons? Your swords."

Malachi chuckled. "Carting them around all the time is likely to get me thrown in jail."

"How do you manage to fight when you don't have them with you?"

"How long will the demon be gone? Do you need help to collect your gear and get out of here before it returns?"

"I'm not leaving. Could you tell which one was the demon? The man or the woman."

He shook his head. "What do you mean you're not leaving?"

Chapter Eight

Esther glanced past Malachi. "Come inside. You'll know if they return, won't you? So you can be gone before they enter the house."

"I don't think you realise how serious this is."

"Can you?"

He nodded.

She stepped back and gestured for him to enter. "I don't have much of a choice."

He came inside. "Are they blackmailing you?"

She closed the door behind him, shaking her head. "It's nothing like that. It's a job." She strode towards her bedroom, stopping at the stairs instead.

"Job?"

She nodded.

"What is more important to you? A job or your life?"

She continued to remain at the base of the stairs,

staring up them. She should have a look up there, but she couldn't bring herself to walk up the stairs. The crackle of fire and smell of smoke filled her mind and she tried to push away old memories.

"Esther."

She turned to him.

"Demons aren't your friend and they never want anything good from humans."

"Never?"

He sighed. "As good as never. Why are you still here? Don't you remember what happened the day we met?"

It wasn't something she'd easily forget. "Of course I remember. And you know that."

"Why are you still here?"

She turned away from the stairs and led the way to her bedroom. She didn't answer him until the door was closed. "I like to eat. And have a roof over my head."

"You can stay with me."

"That isn't going to help me find another job. My resume is terrible enough as it is." She turned away, struggling not to yell at him in frustration.

"You're young enough that a boss wouldn't expect much of a resume," Malachi said. "I'm sure they wouldn't blame you for a lack of job history."

She faced him again, a wry smile forming. "It's not the lack of jobs that's the problem. It's the amount I've been fired from." She strode away from him, pacing the room. "This was meant to be a fresh start. No more fights, no more getting into trouble."

Malachi stepped in front of her, halting her pacing. "Have you considered that it isn't fights you should avoid, but figuring out which ones are worth fighting?"

She stared at him, her gaze roaming his face. When her heart picked up its pace, she reminded herself he wasn't here because he was interested in her. He was worried. "I don't know that I should be taking advice from someone who regularly throws theirself into danger."

Malachi chuckled. "Have you talked to another hunter?"

"No. Why?"

He shrugged. "Never mind then." He paused a moment. "What are you going to do about living with a demon?"

It was her turn to shrug. "I plan to leave in three weeks and three days."

"Why then?" He spoke again before she could comment. "There's a demon outside."

"You have to go." She hurried to the window and

opened it, unlatching the security screen and swinging it inwards. "Hurry. Go before they notice you're here."

"I'll stay nearby in case you need me." He climbed out of the window.

"I won't. Go home."

He stared at her a moment before inclining his head and striding away.

She remained at the window, staring after him, even once he was out of sight. A knock on her bedroom door had her spinning to face it. Fear rushed through her. She was alone in the house with a demon. Hurriedly closing the window and straightening the curtains, she strode to the door, thinking of the cross hidden under her mattress. She half opened the door.

Norman held out a business card. "The fitness centre Elvera wishes you to attend. Do you need a lift?"

She stared at the card. "She wants me to go now?"

"The name of the trainer is listed on the card. She expects you to go at least five days a week." Norman continued to hold out the card.

She reluctantly took it, slipping it in her pocket that also held Elvera's phone. "I'll find my own way there. Probably the best plan since you won't always be able to give me a lift. I'm sure there'll be times when Elvera needs you that will conflict with when I want to go to the fitness centre." She almost grinned at how quickly she came up with the perfect excuse not to get into a car with a demon. Her urge to grin faded as she realised there was no way she could tell Elvera that her employee was a demon. The woman would never believe her.

Norman examined her before he turned away and headed towards the back of the house.

She remained where she was, wondering what he saw when he looked at her. Did demons eat humans? She'd have to ask Malachi. But for now, she needed to ready herself and head to the fitness centre. She glanced at the card. Once she figured out where it was.

It didn't take long to get ready and she was halfway down the street when she saw Malachi's vehicle parked under a shady tree. Her steps slowed. She hadn't expected him to stay. When he got out of the vehicle and remained under the tree, she continued to walk towards him.

"You're okay?" Malachi glanced past her in the direction she'd come from.

"Why are you still here? Why did you stay nearby? I said you could go."

"You don't understand demons and what they're capable of," Malachi said.

She couldn't help thinking about her earlier question. "Do they eat humans?"

"They gain power from human blood."

A shiver ran down her spine. "They…" She shook her head, taking a step back from him. "No." The image of her pricking her finger and letting several drops of blood fall into a glass came to mind.

"How about we go somewhere and talk." Malachi gestured towards his vehicle. "I'm sure you have a lot of questions."

"I can't." She took out the business card. "I'm expected to go here."

Malachi took the card from her, looking it over before he returned it. "I'll give you a lift. We can talk on the way."

She felt like she should protest, but she couldn't get the image of her blood dripping into a glass out of her mind. "Okay." Once she was seated in the vehicle, she leaned back, closing her eyes for a moment. How had her fresh start gone so wrong? Flames banished the image of blood dripping into a glass.

"Did you want to go somewhere else first? Somewhere away from demons," Malachi said.

She opened her eyes to see he looked at her. "You're worried. Why?"

"Some people have a tendency to snap. Demons can be a lot to get your head around."

The images of flames remained in her mind. "There are worse things."

"You've faced other demons. The metaphorical type."

"That's one way of putting it." She turned her head to focus on the street ahead. "Weren't you going to take me to the fitness centre?"

Malachi started the vehicle. "We can help you."

"You and your friends who were with you." She struggled to recall what they looked like. The only images clear from that day were the demons and Malachi.

"The other hunters who were with me. Penelope and Luca. They'd help you too." He pulled out onto the road. "You don't have to do this alone. This is what we've been trained for. To fight demons and protect humans from them."

"It's Norman. He's the demon. That's who came home. Not my boss. Not Elvera." She turned to him. "You could go back there while I'm at the fitness centre." She made a face at the name. "I don't know why they can't just call it a gym and have to get all fancy about it." Everything about this job was too fancy for her. Next time she wouldn't aim so high. She'd get a normal job. And maybe this time she'd somehow manage to keep it for more than a few weeks.

"You want me to go back to the house, while you're gone, and banish the demon," Malachi said.

"That's what you do, isn't it?"

"It's not as simple as that. Has he harmed you in any way? Threatened you?"

"No, but you said demons are evil. Or at least that's the way you've acted when it comes to them."

"Until they harm or threaten a human, I can't banish them to hell."

She stared at him. "What stupid kind of rule is that? And if he's not going to hurt me, why can't I stay?"

"I can return to the house and knock on the door and see what his plans are." Malachi slowed the vehicle, driving into a large car park at the front of a glass-fronted building.

"How will that help? Do you think he's going to tell you he plans to kill a thousand humans and drink their blood?" She tried not to give into the anger that raced through her. "You told me I'm in danger and that you could help me and now you're not interested in doing anything."

"I don't know for certain that you're in danger from Norman, all I know is that he's a demon and they're rarely innocent." He turned off the engine and faced her. "It's safer to avoid demons completely. And since you've already had one bad encounter with them, it's odd that you should be staying in a house with another demon. That's too much of a coincidence for me."

Opening the door, she got out, fighting the urge to hit something. "Do what you want." She strode towards the entrance, ignoring his calls for her to come back.

Stepping inside, the warmth of the temperature controlled building washed over her. Soft music played in the foyer and a woman came forward to greet her, smiling like they were friends who hadn't met in years. She hated the place and immediately wanted to leave. Instead, she returned the insincere smile and explained who she was.

The next couple of hours were boring and tedious, reminding her of why she didn't go to a gym or even deliberately exercise. It also reminded her that she obviously didn't exercise as she discovered muscles she'd forgotten she owned. When she finished her workout, and was given a schedule by the same overly cheerful woman who'd greeted her, she was surprised to find Malachi waited out the front for her.

She hesitated by the door, eventually heading to the vehicle and getting in. "Did you speak to him?"

"I didn't have the chance. He attacked me the moment he opened the door."

"What does that mean?"

"He's been banished to hell." Malachi started the vehicle and backed out of the parking spot.

"So I can return to the house without worrying about demons?"

"There's one demon you don't have to worry about," Malachi said.

"Are there others there?"

"Not that I could tell." He glanced at her. "Esther, demons are dangerous. Do you really want to risk your life like that by staying in a house where demons have resided?"

Before she could comment, a message came through on the phone from Elvera. "Can you drop me in the city? I have a couple of errands to run."

"Has anything I said sunk in?" Malachi asked.

"Yes. But you can't tell me for sure that there is a problem with returning there. Now are you going to take me to the city or do I need to find my own way there?"

He didn't answer immediately. "I can drop you in the city."

Neither of them spoke until they reached the city and Malachi pulled up on the outskirts. "Where do you need to go?"

She reached for the door. "This will do. Thank you." She started to get out of the vehicle.

"I can come with you. Give you a hand and a lift back to where you're staying."

She shook her head. "Everything will be fine. Besides, I'll only be there another three weeks and three days." She started to hop out of the vehicle, stopping again. "Don't wait around for me this time. I'll catch a bus back to the house."

He stared at her a moment before he nodded. "Call me if you need help."

She smiled. "Thank you." It was nice to actually say the words and mean them. Getting out of the vehicle, she closed the door and pulled up a map on her phone so she could find her first destination.

It took her the rest of the afternoon to complete the errands and she barely made it back in time to get ready for dinner. It wasn't until she was at the table that she thought to wonder if there'd been any sign of the fight Malachi and Norman would have had.

There was no time to check now. Elvera wouldn't be impressed if she was late.

Chapter Nine

Finished getting ready, Esther hurried from her room, her steps slowing as she approached the table and saw Norman setting plates down. One in front of Elvera and one in front of the seat for her. Somehow she managed to keep moving and prevent herself from staring at Norman. What had happened? Had Malachi been mistaken?

Slipping into place, Esther kept her gaze on the food in front of her. She wanted to run. Had Malachi mentioned her to Norman? What had happened? The sound of wine being poured into her glass had her glancing up at Norman. He looked the same as always.

Elvera gestured towards the food once Norman had left the table and Esther continued to stare at her plate. "Are you going to eat?"

Thoughts raced through her mind. Incoherent

words and plans that made no sense. Why was she sitting here? Yet what had Norman or Elvera done to her? The woman was overly bossy and Norman didn't say much, but that didn't make them evil.

"Well, Esther?"

Picking up her cutlery, she glanced up to find Elvera watched her. "I'm not that hungry. I'm tired after going to the gym."

Elvera stared silently at her. She gave a single shake of her head before she spoke. "I would not have thought you were so unfit. Contact the trainer and explain you need a faster paced program. You will be fit and healthy within the fortnight." Holding Esther's gaze again, Elvera waited for her to nod before she returned to her meal.

Esther picked at her food and sipped the wine, eventually eating all that was on her plate and drinking the entire contents of the glass. There had been no interruptions or distractions.

Escaping to her room, she readied herself for bed, crawling between the sheets as she sent a message to Malachi. *Why is Norman back?*

I'll pick you up. I can be out the front in twenty minutes.
No.

What do you mean by no? You can't stay there.
She stared at the phone. Was he right? A long

sigh escaped. Things were meant to be different. This was meant to give her a new start. *I'm staying.* She slipped the phone between the mattress and the base, ignoring the vibration of an incoming message. She didn't need his help. She could manage this on her own. Just like she always managed things.

Reaching for the lamp, she turned it off, plunging the room into darkness. Tiredness tugged at her and she stretched out, yawning. Maybe she was more unfit than she thought. Her eyes drifted shut and she thought about the necklace. Her fingers lightly brushed her chest where it would rest if she wore it, her hand stilling and remaining against her chest as she drifted off.

There were no dreams during the night, but she woke in the early hours feeling like she grasped at half forgotten shreds of dreams. They evaporated before she could make sense of them. Moving, she winced at the ache in her head. Why couldn't Elvera drink spirits with dinner? Obviously, wine didn't agree with her.

She stumbled from bed, sinking back onto it when her head spun. That was it. Tonight she'd tell Elvera she hated wine and it didn't agree with her. The thought of standing up to her boss made her groan.

Who was she kidding? She needed this job too much to throw it in over a single glass of wine with dinner.

Staggering to the bathroom, she showered, feeling a little better afterwards. Her head no longer ached so badly. It was now a dull throb. Her stomach was queasy and she felt exhausted, like she hadn't slept at all. Shreds of dreams almost surfaced. They were gone before she could grasp them.

Bright lights? A dizzying array of lights? People? Music? What had her dream been about? She pushed the tantalising images and sounds away. Who cared what she'd dreamt about? It wouldn't help her get through the day. Or through the next three weeks and two days. Straightening her shoulders, she headed for the bedroom door. Reaching it, she remembered the message she hadn't read last night. Hesitating, she nearly returned to check it.

Shaking her head, she left the bedroom, joining Elvera at the table for a silent meal. Norman served them. She sent glances in his direction, trying not to look and have either of them wondering what was wrong with her. She alternated between wanting to warn Elvera that her employee was a demon and wanting to remain silent and stay out of trouble. How many times had speaking up ended badly for her? This was a new start and Norman was none of her business. Besides, Elvera was more than capable of taking care of herself.

The moment breakfast ended, she escaped to her room, dropping onto the bed as she fought against the exhaustion that washed over her. She struggled to sit up, giving in and dropping back against the mattress as her eyes closed.

She had no idea how long she slept, but she was woken by a sound. Checking the time on the phone from Elvera, she saw a message. It reminded her of the one from Malachi. Feeling more rested, she grabbed her handbag and dropped the phone from Elvera in it, slipping her hand under the mattress for the other phone.

Regularly let me know that you're okay.

She slowly shook her head. She didn't need this. *I'm not your responsibility.* She dropped the second phone into the handbag, not waiting for a reply. She had errands to run. And she wasn't about to ask Norman to take her into the city like Elvera had suggested in her text.

She was barely out the door when she noticed the vehicle parked across the road and several doors down. Malachi's vehicle. She strode off in the opposite direction. What did he think he was doing?

She glared at the vehicle when it coasted past and pulled up several metres ahead of her.

The door opened and Malachi stepped out, waiting for her to approach.

"I don't need a babysitter."

"Do you want a lift?" Malachi nodded towards his vehicle.

She crossed her arms over her chest. "Don't you get it? Whatever you tried to do, it didn't help. But it doesn't matter anyway. I don't think Norman is going to be a problem."

"Why are you really staying with them?" Malachi glanced past her, looking in the direction of Elvera's house.

Esther checked over her shoulder, worried Norman might come outside and see her talking with a demon hunter. "You have to leave." She started to step around him.

He held a hand in front of her for a second, temporarily preventing her from moving away. "Do you have a death wish? Or worse?"

She wasn't tempted to ask what worse was. She'd seen it in her nightmares. "I won't be staying there forever. In three weeks and two days, I'll be gone." Again she started to move away from him.

"Gone from the house or gone from this world?"

His words caused her steps to falter. They didn't bring her to a stop. Not much could do that. Not with all she'd experienced.

"Esther."

She didn't answer and didn't look over her shoulder at him.

"Why stay with them? Nothing can be this important that you'd risk your life by staying in a house with a demon."

Images raced through her mind. That was where he was wrong. She didn't want her life to remain as it was. This was her chance to escape to something better. The smell of smoke curled through her memory. The chance to leave old ghosts behind and start over. Yet she didn't tell him. Doubted any words could convince him she could get through this. It was only one more thing to endure. The only difference was that this time there'd be something good to come from enduring it. Not like all the other things she'd endured during her life.

She kept walking, leaving him behind. Reaching the bus stop, she looked up and down the road. Malachi was gone and his vehicle no longer in sight. She was surprised he'd given up so easily. He hadn't seemed the type. The bus pulled up and she entered, vaguely returning the driver's lacklustre greeting as she paid the fare. She sank onto a cold vinyl seat in the middle of the bus, again looking at the street outside. Malachi might be gone, but his words hadn't vanished as easily.

They returned to her over and over throughout the day as she ran seemingly pointless errands. 'Gone from this world.' Who would miss her if she was gone from this world? Who would mourn her like she'd mourned those who were gone?

It was almost a relief to join Elvera at the table that night. She'd spent more than enough time lost in her thoughts. Not that Elvera spoke much. Other than to point out any faults.

Norman interrupted halfway through the meal, remaining silent until Elvera acknowledged him. "The courier has arrived with the paperwork for you to sign. I put him in the library."

Elvera's lips pressed tightly together before she inclined her head and rose to her feet. "He should have been here an hour ago."

"A traffic accident closed the roads he'd chosen to travel on."

"Then he should have walked. There is no excuse for his tardiness." Elvera strode towards the front of the house, Norman following.

Esther barely waited for them to be out of sight

before she grabbed her wine glass and hurried to the kitchen sink, tipping the contents out. She was back at the table and nearly finished her food before Elvera returned.

Elvera remained standing. "Where are your manners? You couldn't wait for me to rejoin you?"

Esther set her cutlery down, not in the mood for Elvera's attitude. "I'm tired. And hungry. If I'd waited I might have fallen asleep."

Elvera looked her over, eventually sitting at the table. "Retire early if you must. Did you contact the trainer today?" She picked up her cutlery. "Maybe you need to be on a multivitamin for your lack of energy."

"I'll pick some up tomorrow." Esther hurried away from the table, not wanting to give Elvera the chance to repeat the first question. She hadn't contacted the trainer. Nor did she want to contact them. She wasn't the type of person to go to a gym. Or a personal fitness centre.

Closing the bedroom door behind her, she leaned against the timber. It was going to be a long three weeks and two days. Sighing, she pushed away from the door and readied herself for bed.

It wasn't until she was about to turn the bedside lamp off that she thought of Malachi. Climbing out of bed, she collected the phone from her handbag and checked for messages. There were none. Was that it? He would leave her alone now? She wasn't sure how she felt about that.

Returning to bed, she slipped the phone under the mattress and turned the light off. Sleep didn't come as easily this time. She drifted in and out, unknown sounds disturbing her. It wasn't until the dreams began that she realised she must have finally fallen asleep. Shadowy, random dreams that made no sense.

Candlelight flickered behind Elvera who lay on the bed beside her, facing her. The woman pressed a finger against her lips, as if hushing her. Then her finger was gone and her face was close.

Esther struggled to wake from the dream. It was impossible. The dream sucked her in, crashing over her and sending her into darkness, the flickering candlelight visible as a moving brightness through her eyelids. A warm breath washed over her lips and then she found herself sitting up and getting out of bed, heading for the stairs that led upwards to Elvera's area.

Reaching the top of the stairs, she rested her hand on the upper railing and walked around the opening that showed the ground floor, heading to a room that was situated at the front of the house. The door on her right was closed, the one on her left open. It contained a king-size bed. She turned her back on the open door and typed a password into the electronic lock beside the closed door. Dazreyella.

A click sounded and she swung the door open, striding inside. On the opposite wall were dark timber filing cabinets, a large metal safe set in the right-hand corner beside them. To the left, along the wall that contained the door, were shelves built into the wall. They were filled with books that looked like they were frequently used. In the middle of the room was an antique desk, a single book set in the middle, a large chair behind the desk facing the doorway.

A sound had her turning to see Norman coming towards her. Stepping in front of her, he held out a manila folder.

She took the folder without a word and strode towards the safe. It too had an electronic keypad, requiring numbers rather than letters. She placed her fingers over the keys.

"Why force yourself to remember that date every time you need to use the safe?" Norman asked.

Chapter Ten

Esther pressed the numbers. One-four-three. She looked towards Norman before she pressed the final number. "Do you think I could ever forget?" Facing the safe, she swung open the door and placed the manila folder on top of various other folders, piles of paper and different types of boxes. There were also several corked bottles on the floor of the safe. She swung the door shut, locking it before facing Norman. "I will never forget." She strode towards him. "Never forgive."

Norman crossed the room, stepping around the desk to stop in front of her. "There are none left to forgive. You saw to that."

Esther felt her lips twist into a smile, one that felt unnatural. She reached out and ran a hand down Norman's cheek. "I have your help to thank for that. It is something else I will never forget."

He captured her hand, clasping it in his. "I would always stand by your side."

Esther looked into his eyes, seeing the fierceness in his gaze. She wanted to step away from him, but her body felt as if it was not at her command. Inclining her head, she drew her hand from his. "Prepare my bath. I wish to soak before we go out." She trailed behind him, stopping at the desk to run her fingers over the cover of the leather-bound book. It was worn and damaged, the pages brittle when she opened to a location partway through, marked by a ribbon. "Norman." She looked up from the book, her fingers remaining against the pages.

He stopped in the doorway, turning to face her.

"You need to increase the dose. It was a struggle tonight."

Norman looked her up and down. "Too much and it could harm rather than sedate."

His words caused panic to rush through Esther. She wanted to demand what he meant. Different words came out instead. "Nothing must go wrong. Only another three nights after this one for me to consolidate my hold. Increase the dose. Both of us can tolerate it."

"Nothing will go wrong. I'll make certain of it."

Norman remained in the doorway a moment longer before he entered the room opposite.

Esther stared after him, eventually lowering her gaze to the book her fingers lightly rested against. There were several hand drawings, the rest of the page filled with slanted, old-fashioned writing. Her fingers were against a drawing of two people lying on their sides, facing each other. Her fingers ran across the page, stopping below the title. Extrication.

Again her lips twisted into a smile. "Not long now." The words were soft as she closed the book, striding from the room and locking the door behind her. Before she could enter the room across from her, Norman stepped out.

"I haven't thanked you yet for having me summoned this afternoon. I appreciate not having to wait the three days it would take to draw me back to this world. Although I am grateful you bound me to your company. It guarantees I'll always be able to return here. There's nothing for me in hell. Only pain."

"You should not have attacked him. The hunters in this town leave demons alone if they don't appear to be doing any wrong." Esther struggled to make herself ask Norman exactly what had happened. The words wouldn't form.

"Why would a hunter have knocked on our door if not to attack?" Norman demanded.

"He probably sensed you while he was driving past. They might not harm demons who appear to be doing no wrong, but they do tend to interfere in things that don't concern them."

Norman lowered his gaze. "I'm sorry my actions caused problems for you."

Elvera gave a dismissive gesture. "I agreed to have Nethod's brother summoned if the two of them track down the hunters. Then there will be no problems turning up on our doorstep."

Norman took a step back. "I will check on the bathwater."

Again Esther found herself watching Norman walk away. She wanted to call him back. Wanted to demand what he'd done to Malachi that afternoon. "Norman."

He stopped and faced her, waiting silently and patiently.

"Bring me some wine. She stirs." She stepped past him and into the bathroom from a previous dream, glancing over her shoulder. "I will take care of the water."

Norman entered the bathroom with a glass of wine as Esther was turning off the taps.

She took the glass from him. "You will change the dose." She had a sip from her glass. "Before the next evening meal."

"Yes, Mistress." Norman strode from the bathroom.

Esther took another sip of the wine, setting it on the edge of the bathtub so she could slip out of her clothes and into the warm water. After another sip, she found it difficult to hold onto the dream and it faded around her.

Pain caused her to wake as she clutched at her head, struggling to sit up. Movement made the pain worse and she breathed in sharply, keeping her eyes closed against the dim, early morning light that made the pain worse. It took a few seconds for the previous night's dreams to crash in on her. They'd felt so real. Dragging herself from bed, she made a grab for the bedside drawers as she stumbled. A drop of wax caught her attention.

She squinted at the wax, running a finger over it. There had been a candle in her dream. She drew in another sharp breath. It had to have been a dream. She picked at the edge of the wax to lift it away from the bedside drawers. The room faded around her, only the wax in focus. Silence filled her ears, a hollow silence that caused the sounds of the stirring neighbourhood outside to vanish. Her hand trembled and she dropped the wax. It seemed to spin endlessly before finally landing on the floor. She didn't reach for it. She remained frozen. If it hadn't been a dream, what had it been?

Had any of them been a dream? Who had she been when she hadn't been herself? Elvera's image came to mind and she came to her feet in a rush. "No." She shook her head, backing away from the drop of wax. "No." Her back collided with the wall and she remained pressed against it, her gaze fixed on the wax. "No." This time the word was little more than a breath of air escaping.

She should have listened to Malachi. The thought had her scrambling for the phone and cross that were tucked under the mattress. With one in each hand, she stared at the wax. This couldn't be real. Images from the dreams tumbled through her mind, all out of order. Her hand against Norman's cheek, sipping the wine, her fingers against the brittle paper, placing the folder in the safe and entering the password for the study. Dazreyella.

A word, or name, that she'd never heard before. She swayed on her feet, her grip tightening on the phone and cross. She had to get out of here. She took a single step towards the door. Again she froze. What if they tried to stop her? Norman was a demon and who knew what Elvera was.

She sank to the floor, still clutching the phone and cross. How had this happened? Things were meant to be different. Was she damned to a life full of near death experiences? She tried to tell herself this wasn't as bad as that night. The night that haunted her dreams. And her nightmares. She didn't really know what was going on. Her gaze was drawn to the phone. She knew someone who might.

Continuing to clutch the cross, she typed in a message and sent it to Malachi. *Is it possible for someone to take over your body?*

The reply came through quicker than she expected. *Where are you? I'll come and get you.*

She wanted to say yes. She had to start thinking and stop reacting. They hadn't harmed her. Yet. She scrambled to her feet. She was pretty certain Elvera had an appointment around mid-morning. She could use that time to escape without either of them knowing. Checking the phone Elvera had given her, she saw that the appointment was at ten. Looking up the address, she calculated that Elvera would probably need to leave around nine.

Esther? You okay? Where are you?

Taking a deep breath, she tried to steady her hands

before she replied. They continued to shake. Being so unsteady had probably been all that had prevented her from running from the house. It had given her the time she'd needed to think things through. *If you haven't heard from me by ten, look for me at my work.*

I'll pick you up now.

No. Not yet. She thought of the room upstairs, the one she knew the password for. She needed to see what else was in there before she left. Had to learn exactly what had been going on.

I will be knocking on the front door at ten.

Okay. She sent the message then thought of a question. *Does the word extrication mean anything to you?*

Where did you hear it? What is going on?

So it doesn't mean anything to you? How about in regards to demons?

It means something. Especially in regards to demons. Removing the human soul from a body in a way to make it possible for another to take its place. Either another human soul or a demon.

She had to read the words over several times. Even then she wasn't sure if this wasn't yet one more nightmare. Hadn't she suffered enough? The smell of smoke and the crackle of fire filled her mind. The heat had been unbearable. The screams worse. And the silence hadn't been any better. So she'd filled the silence with her screams. It hadn't helped. Nothing had.

The phone vibrated, signalling another message, dragging her from old memories. She blinked several times before she was able to focus on the word. *Esther?* Another message came through while she was still reading over the first one. *You okay?*

She slowly shook her head. If she was to tell the truth, it would be that she didn't know when the last time was that she'd been okay. The day before the night that was forever seared into her brain? Or had there been moments since, fleeting ones gone almost as soon as they'd arrived? It certainly wasn't now. She should have known better. It had been a long time since something had gone right for her.

She did what she'd been doing for years, and lied. *Yeah.*

I'll see you at ten.

Okay. The phone remained silent in her hand. Closing her eyes, she tried not to think about the coming meal. How was she meant to sit at the table with Elvera and pretend that nothing had changed? A giggle tried to escape, one she recognised as hysteria. An old friend. It was a strangely comforting feeling.

How many years had she spent pretending things were okay? She could manage to do it for one more meal.

Forcing herself to her feet, she tucked the phone under the mattress, staring at the cross before she did the same with it. As much as she wanted to wear it, she couldn't do anything to alert Elvera.

It didn't take long to get ready for the day and she paced her room, waiting until she could join Elvera for breakfast. Her head didn't ache as much as it had earlier, a shower having helped. She felt exhausted and couldn't help wondering where Elvera had gone last night. Or, where she'd gone with her body. She shuddered at the thought. How was anything like this possible?

Maybe none of her life was real. This could all be some coma induced nightmare from being caught in the fire. She pondered the thought for a moment, almost wishing it was true. Sadly, it wasn't. If it was one thing she'd learned over the years it was the difference between reality and nightmares. She'd suffered more than her fair share of nightmares over the years. Whatever Elvera had been putting in the wine had messed with her ability to recognise the difference, but now she had a bit of an idea of what was going on she knew those dreams hadn't been ones found in sleep.

She checked her phone. It was time. She headed to the table, sitting down at the same time as Elvera. She remained silent as Norman served them, waiting until he left them alone before she spoke. "I've had some of the weirdest dreams since I've been here."

Elvera placed down the fork she'd picked up. "Dreams?"

Esther nodded. "Yes. Dreams. I think it's the wine. I don't normally drink it. I don't think it agrees with me." Rather than examine Elvera's reaction, like she wanted to, she turned her attention to the food, picking up her fork.

"Nonsense. You're obviously nervous about being in a strange place. Give yourself time and you'll settle in."

Esther swallowed her mouthful. "I don't think so. I really think it's the wine." She glanced at Elvera, tempted to smile at the annoyance she could see in the woman's expression. It served her right. Elvera shouldn't have tried to steal her body.

"We'll have a different variety of wine this evening. Although I think you are very much mistaken." Elvera picked up her fork, the conversation clearly ended.

The moment she'd finished eating, Esther rose to her feet. "I hope you don't have any errands for me today. I feel completely exhausted and was thinking of having a nap. I guess those strange dreams have been keeping me from sleeping properly." She met Elvera's gaze, lowering her own after a few seconds. "I can't believe how exhausted I am. Even a full multivitamin didn't help like you suggested." Not that she'd bothered to buy any. But Elvera obviously didn't know that. She focused on the list of things that annoyed her in life in an effort to prevent a smile from escaping. Her previous foster parents were right at the top of that rather long list. Sadness washed over her as she thought about the list of things in life that didn't annoy her. It was a lot shorter.

"I'll be home at midday. I will expect you to be awake by then."

Chapter Eleven

Esther nodded and escaped to the bedroom, leaning against the timber once she'd closed the door. If Elvera left at nine, she'd have less than three hours to learn all she could and escape before she returned. That should be more than enough time. Especially since she knew the password to the room upstairs. A shudder went through her. Why couldn't Elvera have had a bedroom downstairs? It wasn't like she needed both a library and a drawing room. One of them could have been used as a bedroom.

Pushing away from the door, Esther collected the phone and cross, slipping the leather cord over her head before gathering comfortable clothes. Her clothes, not ones bought for her by Norman. She'd just finished changing and slipping the phones into pockets, when her phone vibrated. It was a message from Malachi.

A vehicle left with two people and I can no longer sense a demon in the house.

She hurried to the front door and swung it open, seeing Malachi's vehicle parked on the other side of the road, several houses away. *You can come inside.* Having someone who knew about demons search the place with her would be a good idea. It had nothing to do with her reluctance to go upstairs.

Malachi strode towards her, a cloth backpack slung over one shoulder. The thick, black fabric looked worn and like it had been through the wash quite a few times over the years. It had that well-washed look that a pair of favourite jeans gained.

She returned her phone to the pocket of her jeans, wondering if she should have worn a pair that she didn't care if they were ruined. After all, who knew what to expect upstairs. The crackle of flames echoed in her memory. She forced the sound away, trying to smile in greeting as Malachi reached her.

"Do you need help gathering your things?"

She shook her head, stepping back so he could enter the house. "I want you to have a look at something."

"You're not staying."

She almost laughed at the disbelief in his tone. "I'll

leave after I show you something." She glanced over her shoulder. "It's upstairs."

"Once we have your gear in my vehicle. You don't know when they'll come home." Malachi stepped inside.

"Yes, I do. Midday." She closed the door behind him, leading the way to the stairs.

Malachi tugged her off the first step. "Gear first."

She met his gaze, seeing the determination. "I don't have much. It won't take long to get it."

"Where is your gear?"

She sighed heavily, waiting a moment in the hope he'd change his mind. He continued to meet her gaze, his expression not changing. "Fine. Gear, then upstairs."

As she'd said, it didn't take long to gather her handful of possessions. She almost didn't take any of the new clothes, but changed her mind at the last minute. She needed something to wear to future job interviews. She bundled them up in a thigh-length jacket, using the sleeves to tie it closed. Returning to the house, keeping her handbag with her, she was tempted to sigh heavily again. She started to ask Malachi if he could collect everything useful from the study, including the book that had been on the desk, but decided to wait until he saw the room first.

Closing the front door, she made her way up the stairs, each step an effort. "Is it warmer up here?"

"It feels the same as downstairs." Malachi followed close behind her.

"Are you sure?" She stopped at the top, turning to face him.

He stepped past her, looking around the hallway that curved around the void that showed downstairs. "Yeah." He peered into a bedroom that was across from the stairs. "What did you want to show me?"

Fighting the urge to retreat down the stairs, she strode along the hallway to stop in front of the locked door. Without hesitation, she keyed in the password and opened it.

Malachi nodded towards the keypad. "How did you learn the password? That name sounds demonic. Not something I would have expected you to easily discover."

She tried not to think about how she'd learned it. Basically by being a passenger in her own body. "The hard way." Seeing the book was still on the table, she entered the room and opened it to the ribbon marked location.

"What do you mean by the hard way?" Malachi joined her in front of the desk, turning the book towards him. "How many times have you been possessed? And who was doing the possessing?" He met her gaze. "This is what you wanted to show me?" He rested his hand on the book.

"Yes." She looked away from his penetrating gaze. She didn't want to see his expression when she answered his second question. "Three times." She frowned. "No, I think it's been four times."

Malachi closed the book, shifting it back to the position they'd found it in. "We need to leave. Now. If you've been possessed four times, all it will take is another three for them to evict you from your body."

"What do you mean?" Surely it wasn't the way it sounded. Demon hunters probably had a slang all of their own.

"I'll tell you in the vehicle." He took hold of her hand, trying to tug her towards the doorway.

She drew out of his grip. "I haven't finished looking. You can tell me while I search the place."

"If you knew how much danger you're in, you wouldn't stay here another minute."

She went around to the other side of the desk. "Then why don't you tell me?" She opened each of the three drawers, not finding anything interesting in them.

"What are you looking for?"

She shrugged, moving to the shelves next and

rummaging through the various books and papers shoved in them. She needed to learn more about what was going on. Malachi hadn't exactly given her a great deal of information.

Malachi stepped in front of her and she turned away from the shelves. He captured her hands, preventing her from walking towards the row of filing cabinets. "You being evicted from your body is exactly how it sounds. Without a body, all that awaits is death."

She tried to ignore the unsettling feeling his words caused. "I need to finish searching the room." She tugged her hands from his light grip.

"You don't even know what you're looking for." He followed her to the filing cabinets.

"Then help me look." She opened the top drawer of the first filing cabinet. Finding that it all seemed to be about Elvera's business, she closed it. Drawer after drawer was the same.

Malachi looked up from the bottom drawer of the last filing cabinet. "This is the only drawer that contains anything different. It seems to be dossiers on numerous women who lived at various times during the past several centuries."

She sat on the floor beside him, taking out the two most recent folders. She flicked through the first one, finding a will leaving everything to Elvera. Confusion filled her as she realised the other woman had left everything to her. "What is going on?" She returned the files to the filing cabinet.

"It'd only be a guess, but it seems like these are the many bodies Elvera has previously inhabited." He made a sweeping gesture, encompassing the contents of the drawer before taking out the first file and opening it to the will. "Each of these files will probably contain one of these, leaving it to the woman ahead. All the way through to the last woman in the drawer. Or the equivalent of a will according to the era she comes from."

She scrambled to her feet. Backing away, she slowly shook her head. "There has to be over thirty files in that drawer."

"Around that." He closed the drawer. "One day, there will be a file for you amongst these." He rose to his feet, his gaze never leaving hers.

"You're wrong. This isn't..." Her voice trailed off. "She wouldn't..." Again her voice trailed off. What did she know about demons and extrication other than what Malachi had told her? She returned to the desk to open the book again. She ran her fingers over the sentences, wanting to throw up when different sentences jumped out at her. 'Maintain possession for at least half a night or day.' 'The concoction will not only sedate humans but also loosen the soul's grip on the body.' 'It is important that the seven possessions occur within the space of the full turn of the moon for it to be effective.'

"Esther." He reached for her.

Taking the book, she stepped out of his reach. "It's simple. I leave Brisbane and never come back." She closed the book, shoving it into her handbag. She would read it later. Once she was out of here.

Malachi stepped between her and the doorway. "Has either of them tasted your blood?"

She made a face at the thought. "That's disgusting."

"Have they?"

The urgency in his voice made her want to step back again. She held her ground. "Of course they–" She broke off as an image came to mind. Her blood dropping into a glass. "I don't know."

He stepped forward, reaching for her again. "Esther–"

She stepped out of his reach. "What does that mean?"

He didn't answer immediately. "They will always be able to find you."

She drew in an unsteady breath. "Surely if I went a long way from–"

Malachi interrupted her. "They will always be able to find you."

She wanted to order him to tell her he was wrong. That if she ran far enough, no one could find her. She straightened her shoulders, meeting his gaze. "How do you kill a demon?"

"The simplest is for another demon to do it."

"What about when a demon is in my body? Would that count?"

Malachi chuckled. "And people think I come up with insane plans."

"Then what am I meant to do? Spend the rest of my life running?" How was she meant to be able to afford to do that? She was struggling financially when staying in one place.

"My family will protect you. We'll banish any demon who comes after you."

She wanted to protest. She didn't need anyone to take care of her. She'd been taking care of herself most of her life. She wasn't about to start relying on others to look after her. But she had very little money and nowhere to go. One more day and she would have been given her first pay. Her gaze was drawn to the safe. What had been the number Elvera had used to open it? Surely there were valuable items in it that she could sell.

Malachi followed her to the safe. "What are you doing? We need to leave." He took out his phone and checked the time. "It's a quarter past ten."

She frowned, resting her fingers on the number pad. "We've got plenty of time." She pressed down the first three numbers. One-four-three. "I wasn't watching as she pressed the final number."

Malachi came close. "It's your body. Think about her actions. Your actions. Close your eyes and remember the movements of your fingers."

She did as he suggested, breathing out slowly as she brought back the memory of her body pressing the numbers. She lightly touched the first three again, automatically pressing down the fourth number. "It was seven. One-four-three-seven."

"Fourteen thirty-seven."

She swung open the door of the safe, glancing at Malachi. "What?"

"It was the date on the oldest file. Fourteen thirty-seven. I guess it was a significant year for her."

She rummaged around in the safe, fragments of conversations and comments coming back to her. They made more sense after all she'd learned. "The year she lost her body."

"If she hadn't taken possession of you so many times, we could have used that as a way to get rid of her permanently." He fell silent for a moment. "You're going to steal her money?"

She shoved the small bundle of hundred dollar notes, she'd found at the back of the safe, into her handbag. "Why not? She was going to steal my life."

Malachi chuckled. "I guess she was." His expression became serious when Esther glanced at him. "She still is. That's why we need to leave. Now."

Chapter Twelve

Esther's attention was caught by the folder Elvera had placed in the safe the previous night. She took it out and started to open it. "Do something other than watch me search the safe." She drew in a sharp breath as she read the words along the top of the first piece of paper inside the folder. Last will and testament.

"There isn't exactly anything to do around here. What we should be doing, is running. And not looking back."

She made a vague gesture, as if waving him away. "Count the folders in the bottom drawer of the last filing cabinet. Do something useful." The rest of the words she would have spoken vanished from her mind. Elvera was leaving everything to her? Shock raced through her. It was all true. She was the next body Elvera planned to steal. Anger followed on the heels of the shock and her grip tightened on the folder, crumpling the light cardboard. It was her body. And she wasn't about to give it up without a fight.

"Thirty-two."

She looked down at Malachi as he closed the filing cabinet drawer. "What?" For a moment she had no idea what he was talking about, then it hit her.

"The amount of bodies she's stolen." Malachi rose to his feet, his gaze continuing to hold hers. "She's been doing this for centuries and getting away with it."

Esther closed the folder with a snap and shoved it inside her handbag, her fingers brushing against the leather cover of the book. "She picked on the wrong person this time."

Malachi grinned at her. "I guess you found something worth fighting about."

A wry smile twisted her lips. "The fights usually are about me. Or my attitude at least."

Malachi laughed. "Is that why you're being contrary and staying when you should be leaving?"

"I'm not being contrary." She glared at him before she returned to searching the safe.

"What more do you want out of there? The entire contents?"

Her smile returned. This time it was filled with

humour. "Possibly." She grabbed some of the papers and shoved them in her handbag along with three of the smaller wooden boxes. They looked of a size suitable to store necklaces. The kind of necklaces consisting of large jewels. "Let's go then." She pushed the safe door closed. "I want to put some distance between us and this house."

Malachi led the way, stopping at the top of the stairs.

Esther ran into him. "What are you-" She broke off when she stepped around him, spotting Norman at the foot of the stairs. The crackle of flames echoed in her mind and the hallway became uncomfortably warm. "Oh." She wanted to ask Malachi what the options were, but Norman would hear them too. She also had the fleeting urge to apologise to Malachi for not leaving earlier.

"Did one of our enemies send you to us?" Norman glanced at Malachi, returning his attention to Esther. "Or was it hunters?"

"I wanted the job. But I'm not about to give up my life to get it." Esther's hands curled into fists. "Out of the way."

"I can't do that. You belong to Elvera."

A shiver ran through her. "I don't belong to anyone. Now get out of my way."

Malachi drew a dagger out of his boot. "Step back, Esther." He kept his gaze on Norman. "I can return you to hell as many times as necessary."

Her mouth dropped open when Norman formed a sword out of nothing, striding up the stairs towards them. She doubted a dagger could compete with a sword. Nor was she about to get trapped upstairs. Ducking, she threw herself forward to tackle Norman around the legs. Before she could tumble down the stairs with him, she was dragged back by her handbag strap.

Malachi let go of the handbag the moment she regained her balance. "I'll meet you in the vehicle." Before she could protest, he ran down the stairs and attacked Norman who'd gained his feet.

She hurried after him, looking around for a weapon. She was over running from fights. That wasn't her. It looked like all running did was put her in more danger than usual and would probably get her killed. She'd take a messy life against a meek one any day.

"Outside," Malachi ordered.

She didn't see anything that would make a suitable weapon. Or an unsuitable one. "I'm not about to let you fight my battles."

Malachi continued to attack Norman. "I'll follow."

The words froze her in place for a moment as she heard the echo of other words. Similar ones. 'Run, Esther. Don't look back. We'll follow.' They hadn't. It had already been too late. If she'd known, would she have stayed and tried to help them?

"Esther. Run!" Malachi was kept too busy fighting Norman to look in her direction. "Hurry."

Before she could protest, two demons burst in the back door, running towards them. Esther's heart raced. It was Nethod and his brother. It took her a moment to remember the second demon's name. Torrnon.

"About time. I called you the moment Elvera realised someone had entered her study. You should have arrived before me." Norman continued to attack Malachi.

"This isn't our fault," Nethod said. "You brought this about with your plans for the girl. You're also the ones who got us caught up in this situation."

Esther slowly backed towards the front door, trying to figure out what she could do. She hated feeling helpless.

"I refuse to have this discussion again. Get over here and help," Norman demanded.

Malachi blocked, barrelling into Norman when the other two demons came closer. He spun, grabbing

Esther's hand and dragging her with him to the front door.

She ran at his side, willing to leave now he was with her. Glancing over her shoulder, she stumbled. The demons were following.

Nethod grinned at her. "Running won't help. I'll be tasting your sweet blood again shortly."

An image of her blood dripping into a wine glass came to mind. This time though, the glass was nearly full. She struggled to push the image from her mind. With the demons gaining on them, it was nearly impossible.

Reaching the vehicle, Malachi flung the door open. "Get in the back."

She did as he directed, not wanting to waste the time to run around the vehicle to the passenger front seat. She was still closing the door when Malachi drove off. She struggled to put her seatbelt on as Malachi took a corner fast, slamming her against the door. Relief rushed through her that she'd managed to get it shut in time. Buckled up, she twisted in her seat to see where the demons were. The street behind them was empty. "We've lost them."

"No, we haven't. The one who has tasted your blood can follow. And the blood enhanced link Elvera has with you will allow her to find you. We need to keep moving until we can come up with a better plan."

"We're going to stay in the vehicle?" Esther eyed the limited space in the back. It would get pretty cramped fairly quickly. "We won't be able to get out at all?"

"I need to drop into my house first. Pick up a few things and make some calls."

Sitting directly behind him, she was able to see the dagger on the front passenger seat. "If you can't kill them, what use is a dagger against demons?"

"As a tool to both defend and help return them to hell." Malachi glanced in the rear view mirror, momentarily meeting her gaze. "It's preferable to standing around and letting a demon kill me."

"How do you use one to send them to hell?" She needed to know everything about demons. There had to be some way of getting rid of them. And especially getting rid of the four that were after her.

"One of the things I want to collect from my house is a book written by an ancestor of mine. 'Demonology'. It'll help answer some of your questions."

She looked out the back window again. As far as she could tell, there were no demons following. But for all she knew, they could be in one of the other vehicles on the road. "How far are we from your place?"

"Fifteen to twenty minutes, depending on the traffic." He paused a moment. "There's no point checking over your shoulder. You won't spot them in the traffic."

Before she could argue that it would be impossible to stop checking, her phone rang. The one Elvera had given her. She rolled down the window, taking out the phone. She stared at the name on the screen. How could everything have ended up in such a mess? She wound the window down.

"What are you doing?" Malachi asked.

She looked from the phone to the open window. She lowered her hand, turning the phone off instead. So much for not reacting to situations in the future. She really had to start thinking first. Maybe then she'd end up in less messes. "I have absolutely no idea."

Malachi turned off the busy street he was on and onto a quieter one. "We'll be at my place shortly. We can take a few minutes to plan our next step when we arrive."

She looked out the back window again. She didn't bother telling Malachi it wouldn't help. How could she come up with a plan when she had no idea what to do about any of it. She didn't want to die. The memory of screams echoed in her mind. Would her end be as painful?

Malachi pulled up in front of a lowset house. It was red brick, blending in with the rest of the houses in the neighbourhood. He stopped in front of the closed garage door, turning off the ignition and collecting the dagger from the passenger seat. He looked over his shoulder. "You okay?"

She had no idea what to say. Her gaze was drawn to the phone she continued to hold. "Can we win?" She met his gaze when he didn't immediately answer. "Can we?"

"I guess that depends on what you consider winning."

She thought of and discarded several answers before she settled on one. "Surviving."

Malachi grinned. "Easily done."

She remained in the seat while he got out, trying to decide if she believed him. Eventually, she decided it didn't matter. She wasn't about to let Elvera beat her. She reached for the door handle. The door swung open before she could make contact.

Malachi smiled down at her. "I promise not to bite." His smile widened into a grin. "Unless of course you ask nicely."

She was reassured by the humour she could see in his eyes. "How do you do that?"

"Do what?" He held a hand out to her, stepping back slightly.

"Smile. In the face of all this danger." She took his hand, even though she didn't need his help to get out of the vehicle.

He chuckled. "That's the fun part." After lightly squeezing her hand, he let go and led the way to the front door. It was set back from the front of the house, creating a small, sheltered area.

She followed him inside. The room was open plan with the kitchen to the far left, a dining table in the middle and a lounge suite clustered around a television on a low cabinet to the right. In the front right corner, was a single door leading out of the room. It was neat, tidy and had very little personality. "How long have you lived here?"

Malachi chuckled. "My family keeps telling me I need to make the place look less drab, but I'm rarely home. Too busy chasing demons." He gestured towards the door on the right. "Bathroom is second door along the hallway if you need it. I'll grab some things and be ready to leave shortly."

"Thanks." She entered the hallway, slowing as she passed the first open door. She came to a halt when she saw the weapons on display. Some were locked in mesh cages while others were on various types of racks or stands. She took one step into the room. This was obviously where he spent time when he was home. There was also a bench that ran along the far wall, locked cabinets beneath it, various daggers displayed on top of it. What she couldn't get over was the variety. Daggers, swords, bows, spears and things she had no idea what they were.

Malachi joined her, chuckling. "I forgot this door was open. I'm surprised it didn't send you running."

She turned to face him, very little space between them. "Do you know how to use all these weapons?"

"Some better than others."

"And you've used them against demons."

He nodded.

"Teach me."

His gaze remained on her face as he scrutinised her. "You're serious."

"Yes."

"Why?"

"Because I'm not about to sit back and wait for them to kill me." Her hands tightened into fists. "Or find me."

Malachi grinned. "Sounds good to me. It's always

better to choose the battleground rather than be surprised on some unknown turf."

"So you'll teach me?"

"No. I–"

She interrupted him. "Why not? I'll follow whatever rules you set. Anything. Please, Malachi."

He captured her hands when she reached for him. "I'm not a good teacher. But I know someone who is."

Chapter Thirteen

It took a second for Malachi's words to sink in. Ester's gaze was drawn to his hands clasped around hers. "Sorry." She tugged her hands from his grip.

"What are you sorry for?"

She took a step back from him, moving further into the room. "I shouldn't have hassled you like that. It's just…" She looked away from him, not wanting to finish the sentence. She'd spent more than enough of her life confronted by death.

"It's okay." He followed her into the room, glancing past her. "The book I was going to lend you is in the far cupboard at the end of the bench. It isn't locked."

"Oh." She'd thought he'd come to check on her. She stepped to the side. "I didn't manage to make it to the bathroom." She gave a half smile. "I won't be long." She hurried along the hallway, feeling awkward and idiotic. In the bathroom, she stared at herself in the mirror over the vanity. Her cheeks were flushed.

She'd nearly thrown herself at him, begging him to help. Which seemed rude considering all he'd done so far was help her. She used the toilet while she was in the bathroom, washing her face when she was finished, trying to convince herself that she had everything under control. Like always, she was far from having a single thing sorted. Her life was its typical mess. A different mess, but a mess none the less.

Esther found Malachi by the dining table, placing a book and several weapons on it. There was another well-worn cloth backpack already on the table. It appeared to be slightly older looking than the other one Malachi used.

He looked over at her. "You ready to go?"

Esther opened her mouth to answer. A knock on the door prevented her from saying anything. Her heart raced and she spun to face the door.

There was another knock at the door. "Malachi."

She didn't recognise the masculine voice that called out, so at least it wasn't Norman or Elvera. "Who is it?" Esther kept her voice low.

"One of my cousins. I forgot Blake was coming

over." Malachi strode towards the front door, swinging it open.

Seeing two strangers, Esther hung back. Annoyance arrowed through her. It wasn't like her to remain in the background, worried about what would happen. She joined Malachi by the front door, looking over both his guests.

The young man had blue eyes, dark hair and tanned skin, his hair looking like it needed a trim and as if it had been a few days since he'd last shaved. The slightly scruffy look suited him. He had his arm draped around the shoulders of the young woman beside him. She had green eyes and her dark hair fell in layered waves past her shoulders. A crimson streak curved through it from the crown of her head to mingle with the dark strands on her left. They were both dressed in black jeans and long sleeved shirts, crosses at their necks identical to the one Malachi wore.

"This is my cousin Blake and his partner Allie," Malachi said.

Allie held out her hand. "You must be the one Malachi has been worried about."

Shaking Allie's hand, she glanced at Malachi. "I doubt it." There was no reason why he'd be worried about her. He barely knew her.

Malachi stepped back. "Come in. I forgot we had plans for this arve. I was going to visit Father Joe. I'm out of holy water and I need some for Esther."

Blake took two vials out of a pocket, handing them over. "It's not like you to run out."

"I've had a few busy days. Between clean up duties and getting rid of a demon for Esther." Malachi put one of the vials in a pocket of his jeans.

Allie was the last one to enter the house, closing the door behind her. "Did you really forget you were meant to be checking hallowed ground with us or was it deliberate? I don't blame you if it was deliberate. It doesn't sound like it's going to be much fun. I'd rather be out fighting demons than visiting churches and graveyards."

Esther looked between Allie and Malachi, trying to make sense of the conversation.

Malachi strode to the kitchen. "I can probably check out the places that are furthest from here. We need to keep on the move so it could work in well with our plans." He took a glass out of the cupboard and a quarter filled it with water, tipping a vial of holy water into it.

Blake shrugged. "We can manage if you want to get further out of the city." He headed towards the hallway, glancing over his shoulder. "I'll grab a bucket from the laundry."

Malachi strode towards Esther. "Take a seat. Either the lounge or dining chairs. It doesn't matter."

"Of course it matters," Allie said. "She's going to be throwing up. If it was me, I'd want to be sitting on one of the dining chairs."

Esther backed away from Malachi. "Throwing up?"

Blake returned to the room in time to hear Esther's words. "I guess a demon has drunk your blood. If they haven't had much, it won't be too bad."

"It's always bad," Allie muttered.

Esther made her way unsteadily to a dining chair, not sure she wanted to find out exactly what was going on. She held up a hand when Malachi tried to hand the glass to her. "What happens if I don't drink it?"

Malachi placed the glass on the table beside Esther. "I know you barely know me, but I need you to trust that I wouldn't do anything to hurt you. That I will do my best to protect you from the demons hunting you down."

She looked up at him, surprised at how sincere he sounded. "Why?"

Allie came closer. "They helped me too. It's what their family does. Have done for centuries."

Esther frowned. "You were hunted by demons?"

Allie grinned. "You could say that." When Esther started to speak, she interrupted. "Long story. You won't have time for it now."

Blake held the bucket out to her. "Break your tie to the demon who has consumed your blood."

"Extrication," Malachi said.

Blake stared at Malachi for a moment, continuing to hold out the bucket. "I haven't heard that word in a long time."

Allie looked from Blake to Malachi. "What is going on?"

Esther took the bucket from Blake, almost relieved to find that she knew more than someone else about the situation for a change. "A demon wants my body, minus me."

"They want to kill you?"

"Sort of. Not exactly though. From what I've figured out, she plans to kick me out because she needs a new body for herself." She smiled at Allie's horrified expression. "That's kind of how I feel about it too."

Allie grabbed hold of Blake's arm. "We're not going to let that happen, are we?"

"I'm trying to avoid it." Malachi gestured towards the glass. "Are you going to drink the holy water?"

She eyed the glass, picking it up and drinking it in one mouthful. The contents had barely gone down when they were coming back up, pain exploding through her body. She stared at the blood in the bottom of the bucket, trying to ignore the pain that filled her body. It had eased off, but not enough. "Is that normal?"

Allie made a face. "Yeah. At least it was only a couple of teaspoons worth of blood. Mine was worse."

Blake took the bucket from her. "I'll deal with this."

Esther started to rise from the chair. "I can-"

Malachi pressed against her shoulder. "We need to make sure no demon can use the blood against you."

"I'll help." Allie followed Blake from the room.

Malachi gathered the gear from the table. "I'll be back in a minute. I'll put everything in the vehicle."

Esther was left alone in the room, trying not to think about the latest mess her life was in. Why did things like this always happen to her? She rummaged in her handbag, taking out the items she'd stolen from Elvera and placing them on the table. An old book, a small pile of paper that was bent and crumpled from being in her bag, a folder and three timber boxes. She opened the boxes first, hoping they contained something she could sell. The money Norman had given her wasn't going to last long. Nor would the money she'd taken from the safe last forever.

She stared at the dagger in the first box. It was curved and made of a polished black material. Cautiously running a finger along the side of the blade, she frowned. It was made of stone? Opening the other two boxes, she found identical daggers in them. With the way her life was going, she should have known they would be useless.

Blake and Allie returned to the room, Allie coming over to the table to pick up one of the daggers. "Where did you get the demonic weapons? And so many of them."

Esther looked up at Allie. "Demonic weapons? Like made from demons or something?"

Blake picked up a dagger, examining it. "As in from hell. Brought with them to our world."

Esther picked up the dagger she'd run her finger across. "These came from hell?" They felt ordinary. Or at least they didn't feel like they came from somewhere like hell. Another thought occurred to her. "Is there a heaven too?"

Allie shrugged, placing the dagger in the box. "We can only assume."

Malachi joined them at the table, taking the dagger from Esther and returning it to the box. "Don't play with demonic weapons." He turned to Blake. "What were you doing letting her play with that?"

Blake chuckled, putting the dagger he examined, back in the box. "Look at you being responsible for a change."

Esther looked from Blake to Malachi. "Responsible for a change?"

Allie laughed softly when Malachi looked uncomfortable. "A taste of your own medicine?"

"It's different when you're the one doing the worrying rather than being the one others are worried about," Blake said.

Malachi began to gather the items Esther had placed on the table. "We should probably go. We don't want to be caught by Elvera." A piece of paper drifted out of the pile.

Esther grabbed hold of it before it could land on the floor. She started to return it to the pile. Several words caught her attention. "A doctor's report?" She frowned. "Elvera has a heart problem that can't be fixed?"

Malachi took the paper from her. "Or they've set up the reason for her death so she, or your body, isn't blamed since you're her heir."

A shudder ran through Esther and she took the

piece of paper from Malachi, adding it to the pile. "That is not going to happen."

"There's only one way to prevent that," Blake said. "Elvera must die."

"Can't I just avoid her?" Esther rose to her feet. "If she can't find me, she can't steal my body."

Blake shook his head. "She's already started the process. Unless you die, she can't take over another body."

She wanted to sit back on the chair she'd vacated. Her legs felt like they might not hold her up. "I have to kill her?"

"It doesn't need to be you." Blake's words were soft, his expression sympathetic.

She couldn't hold his gaze. Looking away from him, she tried not to think about the situation. Why had she tried to make a new life? She should have known it would fail. "We should go." Standing around wasn't helping. It was only letting her know how screwed up her life was. And the news was getting worse by the minute. Who knew what they'd tell her if they remained here any longer.

Allie momentarily rested a hand on Esther's arm. "We'll help. You're not in this salone."

She met Allie's gaze, not sure how she felt about that. "Being alone doesn't bother me. I'm used to it."

"Not anymore." Allie turned towards Malachi. "If you want to help check for hallowed ground, I can send you part of the list."

"Yeah, we'll check places well away from here." Malachi led the way to the front door once everything was back in Esther's handbag. He glanced over his shoulder at Esther, who followed. "Can you drive?"

She nodded as she followed him out the door, Blake and Allie behind her. "Why?"

"We can take turns to drive and sleep later. Keep on the move so they can't find us."

Chapter Fourteen

After saying goodbye to Allie and Blake, Esther joined Malachi in his vehicle, sitting in the front passenger seat. "We can't drive forever."

"Only until we figure out what to do." Malachi started the vehicle, reversing out onto the street, passing a four-wheel-drive parked out the front.

She had no idea what to do. "Where is the book you said I should read?"

Malachi nodded towards the back seat. Before he could say anything, his phone made a noise, indicating an incoming message. He handed the phone over to Esther. "That should be from Allie."

She checked the message. "It's a list of churches and graveyards." She frowned. "The message says to do them in this order, but they seem to be all over the place." Or at least it seemed that way to her from what little she knew about the different suburbs.

Malachi chuckled. "That should make it hard for them to keep track of us." He gestured towards the GPS. "Put in the address for the first one."

After she'd put in the address, she twisted in her seat to reach the book that was on the back seat with the other items Malachi had brought out. Except for the weapons. She had no idea where they were. That made her think of the daggers in her handbag. She really didn't want a cop to find them in there. She doubted that would go down well. But she had nowhere else to leave them.

Once she was facing forward, she opened the book and began to read, avoiding looking too closely at the demon on the front of the cover. She had enough nightmares without gaining more images to add to them.

The afternoon was spent reading and visiting the various locations Allie had sent them. Malachi messaged Blake after each location, letting his cousin know the place didn't need to be blessed.

As the sun set, they pulled up in front of another graveyard. The old headstones, visible through the broad limbed trees, were crumbling from age. Esther set the book aside, getting out of the vehicle. "How do you know they don't need to be blessed?"

"The same way I know demons are in an area."

He glanced at his left wrist. "My demon mark." He started to get out of the vehicle, pausing to take out his phone when it rang. He glanced at the screen before answering. "Talitha." He chuckled. "No more than usual." There was another pause before he spoke again. "You know I would." He got out of the vehicle, still on the phone. "You too."

Esther joined him in front of the vehicle, waiting until he'd put his phone away before she spoke. "Is everything okay?"

Malachi used the central locking. "Yeah. That was one of my sisters. The one closest to me in age."

"Older or younger?"

"They're both older." He led the way into the graveyard.

"What's it like? Having siblings."

"Like anything in life, it's both good and bad." He strode towards the middle of the cemetery.

"In what way?"

"They always have my back, but they also know the best ways to annoy me." He grinned. "That works both ways."

"How many siblings do you have?"

"Only two sisters. Talitha and Jerusha. I also have a lot of cousins who are as close as siblings to me."

She had cousins. "Maybe it's a good thing I don't have siblings if they're anything like cousins."

Malachi chuckled. "All families are different." He stopped in the middle of the cemetery, doing a slow turn as he scanned the area.

She did the same, still no closer to figuring out what it was he searched for each time. "How does all this work?"

"What exactly?"

"Demons and stuff. And how do you know what to do?"

Malachi shrugged. "It just does. And I've been training my entire life to be a hunter."

"Did you ever want to do anything different?"

"Never." Reaching the vehicle, Malachi unlocked it, remaining at the front of it as he looked down the street.

She looked in the direction he stared in, remaining by the vehicle door. "What's wrong?"

"Wait here." Slipping the keys back into his pocket, he strode away from the vehicle.

She started after him, not having any idea of why he'd walked off so abruptly.

He glanced over his shoulder. "Wait in the vehicle. There are demons in the area."

"I'm not about to stay by myself if there are demons

nearby. What if they come after me? How am I meant to fight a demon? I don't know enough about how to do it. From what I've read of your ancestor's book, I'm going to die a horrible death."

"All the more reason for you to stay in the vehicle and not go running into danger." He chuckled. "Not a comment I would have expected to make."

"Why do you care?"

He glanced at her. "Why shouldn't I?"

She began to push for an answer, the words evaporating when she saw the two demons walking towards them. It was Nethod and Torrnon. It looked like she could stop worrying about how to recognise any demons in the area. These two she knew a little too well.

Malachi stepped in front of her, stopping. "I can deal with them. You go back to the vehicle."

She peered around his shoulder. "There's two of them."

Malachi glanced around the area before drawing two daggers from his boots. "You're right, it's a little unfair on them."

A smile reluctantly formed. She recognised the attitude. No wonder she got along so well with him. "In that case, there's no reason I should retreat."

"All right then. Let's return these two to hell." He strode forward, his daggers ready.

She followed several steps behind him. "What if someone sees us and calls the cops?" She looked up and down the road. The neighbourhood was full of large trees, some of them dimming the light from the overhead streetlights.

"Most people don't notice what goes on around them. If any do notice, we'll be out of here before the police can respond."

Nethod stopped in front of them, a sword in one hand and his claws looking as dangerous as his weapon. He glanced at his brother who also carried a sword. "The human is right. They will be out of here before the police can respond. Out of this life."

Torrnon grinned, showing his rows of teeth. "Unless we decide to play with them. Don't you love it when they scream?"

Fear rushed through her at the difference in size between the weapons Malachi held compared to those the demons used. "What can I do to help?" Her gaze remained fixed on Torrnon's sword. It looked more dangerous than the one his brother wielded.

"I don't suppose you know the Lord's prayer." He attacked Nethod, blocking Torrnon when he tried to go after Esther.

"How will that help?" She'd been forced to say it more times than she liked to think about.

"Trust me."

Torrnon got past Malachi, swinging his sword at Esther who stumbled backwards. She started reciting the prayer, dodging the weapon. It didn't help. She stumbled over the edge of the gutter, sprawling across the footpath. Torrnon grabbed her arm, dragging her to her feet, his claws breaking her skin. She struggled to escape, the words of the prayer failing her.

"Esther, keep praying." Malachi tried to get past Nethod who prevented him from reaching Esther and Torrnon.

"Let me go." She elbowed Torrnon. It made no difference.

The demon wrapped his other arm around her waist, his sword clattering to the ground. "We'll be well rewarded for returning you." He let go of her arm, bringing his bloodstained claws to his lips.

Pain exploded through her and she tried not to scream, a gasp escaping. She wasn't about to give Torrnon the satisfaction of hearing her scream. Nor did they want to draw any attention. The last thing they needed was the cops turning up and finding the weapons they both carried. Weapons! She struggled to escape, plunging a hand into her handbag, trying to find a dagger amongst all the items.

"So sweet." The demon ran a claw along her cheek, a fine line of blood forming on her skin. "So very sweet."

Pain exploded through her again as he consumed the blood from his claws. Her hand wrapped around one of the boxes and she slipped it open, gasping again when she cut her hand on the dagger. Drawing it from her bag, she stabbed it into the demon who let go of her with a howl. Spinning to face him, she returned to reciting the prayer, throwing herself at the demon.

"Run, Esther. Don't bother attacking. Just run," Malachi ordered.

Torrnon escaped her grip, taking a step towards his sword.

Esther ignored Malachi, not having the time to check and see what he was doing. Transferring the dagger to her other hand, she slashed at Torrnon, digging in her bag for a second dagger. She found it, this time not cutting herself when she drew it out. Not that it made any difference. The blood from her earlier cut left bloody prints on the blade, making it glisten in the limited streetlight.

"Where did you get them from?" Torrnon backed away from the two daggers.

Esther grinned. "Don't tell me you're worried about these little things."

"You're an executioner?" Torrnon took another step towards his sword, glancing between it and Esther.

She wanted to ask him what that meant, but she needed to do something before he could reach his sword. She threw herself at him, sinking both daggers into his body.

He howled, trying to escape her grip.

Drawing out one of the daggers, she stabbed him again, continuing with her recitation of the prayer. When he howled, she once more withdrew the dagger, plunging it into where his heart would be if he was human. She had no idea if demons had the same anatomy, but thought it worth trying. She couldn't hold him much longer. Not with how he struggled to escape.

Torrnon vanished with one last howl, calling out his brother's name.

Esther landed on the ground, trying not to cut herself again on a dagger, a sharp burning pain slashing across her wrists. She started to check them, having felt certain the daggers hadn't been anywhere near her wrists.

Nethod roared, barrelling past Malachi. "I will kill you for that. I don't care what Elvera wants. You will be as cut from this existence as my brother has been."

Esther put up an arm to block the coming attack, knowing she'd never gain her feet in time.

Malachi tackled Nethod, Esther's dagger scratching the demon's skin before the two of them crashed to the ground. "Leave her alone or you can join your brother." He struggled to keep hold of Nethod.

"There's nothing to join." Nethod wrestled with Malachi. "Don't you understand? She severed all his ties to existence. She executed him."

Esther scrambled to her feet. "You're next." She tightened her grip on the blood coated daggers.

Before Esther could reach him, Nethod twisted out of Malachi's grip. "I'm not about to drink the blood of an executioner. Torrnon wouldn't have either if you hadn't hidden what you are."

Esther stalked towards Nethod as Malachi rose to his feet, picking up one of his daggers he'd dropped during the fight. She smiled at Nethod, refusing to let the demon see how terrified she was. Or how little she knew. "A lot of the blood on my hands is mine. I'll force it into you and then execute you."

Nethod backed away, pointing a finger at her. "This isn't over. You will pay for what you've done." Gathering up the two swords, he rushed away from them, quickly lost from sight.

Esther stared in the direction Nethod had taken. "What just happened?"

Malachi sheathed his daggers. "I don't know."

"What do you mean you don't know?" Esther lowered her hands, wishing she could clean the blood off them and put the daggers away.

Malachi's gaze focused on the daggers. "We need to find out more about them. And I can think of one person who might be able to tell us what they are." He took a step in the direction of the vehicle. "Let's get you and the daggers cleaned up then I'll send a picture of them to my gran."

Chapter Fifteen

"Your gran?" Esther nearly demanded what some old lady would know about weapons and fighting. Then it dawned on her that Malachi had said his family were hunters. "Your gran fights demons?"

Malachi chuckled. "You don't have to sound so shocked. My family have been fighting demons for centuries. She's my oldest family member and is actually my great-aunt. She was my great-grandmother's younger sister. Most of us call her Gran though. She's the last one left of her generation." He stopped at the back of the vehicle, opening the boot.

"That's sad." She knew what it was like to be the last one left.

"She has plenty of family, but yeah, she probably misses her parents and siblings." He took a bottle of water from the boot. "Hold out your hands. After I wash the blood off I'll sprinkle the ground with holy water and salt where the water falls."

"Why?"

"So no demon can use your blood against you."

She tried not to think about all the blood she'd lost throughout her numerous fights over the years. "Why hasn't any demon gone after my blood before? It's not like I've been careful about it."

"Most times they'll ignore dried blood, but they make an exception for hunters and those they're already going after." Finished washing the blood from her hands and the daggers, Malachi returned the bottle of water to the boot. He opened a container of salt and sprinkled it across the damp ground before using the vial of holy water Blake had given him.

Esther started to put the daggers away.

Malachi held out a hand, the salt already back in the boot. "Wait. I'll take a photo of them." He closed the boot. "Put them here." He took out his phone, turning the flash on before he took a photo of the daggers Esther had placed on the boot lid.

She waited until he finished before returning the daggers to their boxes. "What if your gran doesn't know anything about them?"

"She'll consult our library of books on demons." He headed for the driver's door.

Esther waited until she was seated before she continued speaking. "Your family owns a library?"

Malachi chuckled. "You could say that." He pulled out onto the street, his phone signalling a message. He handed the phone over to Esther after glancing at the screen. "Read it out to me."

She opened the message. "She wants to know where you found them."

"Tell her we took them from a demon and there are three of them."

She sent the message, staring at the screen as she waited for a reply. The screen darkened before a message came through. "She wants you to visit."

"Tell Gran we have demons tracking us."

Once more she sent the message. It didn't take as long for a reply to come through. "She wants to see you immediately."

"We're about twenty minutes away."

Esther sent the message then lowered the phone. "What if Elvera and Norman turn up at your gran's place?"

Malachi chuckled. "We pity them. Gran might be old, but she'd still take on any demon who came after her."

When silence fell, she took the book 'Demonology' from her handbag. It was taking longer to read than she'd expected considering the size of the book. But she'd read back over sections, wanting to make sure she understood everything. She didn't know how she'd manage it, but she wasn't about to let Elvera take over her body again. It was hers and she wasn't about to be extricated. She couldn't stop thinking about the daggers and if she'd somehow taken the solution with her when she'd escaped from Elvera's.

Malachi pulled up in front of a spacious house nestled in a garden that looked like it might be filled with flowers during spring and summer. The house was timber and painted in creams and browns. Malachi stopped beside another vehicle in front of closed double garage doors. He stared at the other vehicle for a moment before he turned off the engine.

"Whose is it?" Esther put the book aside, nodding towards the vehicle.

"It belongs to one of my cousins." Malachi swung open the door.

Esther rested a hand on his arm when he would have got out of the vehicle. "You don't like them?"

Malachi grinned at her. "She's one of my favourite cousins."

"Then why did you hesitate?"

"It wasn't anything to do with Scarlett. Or her

partner. Or at least nothing negative about either of them."

"But it is bad?"

"I don't know. If Gran has asked Jesse to be here, maybe the daggers are outside what she knows."

"Jesse?"

Malachi grinned again. "Some things have to be seen to be believed." He pulled away from her, getting out of the vehicle.

She walked with him to the front door, wanting to take a step back when it swung open at their approach. A young woman stood in the doorway. She had warm brown eyes, a wiry frame and short blond hair that feathered around her fine boned face. A demon mark disappeared beneath the long sleeve of her black shirt.

"Did Gran ask you to be here?" Malachi asked.

The young woman nodded, turning to Esther. "I'm Scarlett." She held out her hand.

Esther shook it, noticing the small gold cross on a leather necklace at her throat. "Esther."

Scarlett stepped back, gesturing for them to enter. "Gran said she'd join us shortly. Jesse is waiting in the lounge room."

Esther entered the house, leaving her shoes with the rest of the ones beside the door when Malachi removed his. She glanced around the foyer. There were two closed doors to her left, one straight ahead and an open doorway on her right. Scarlett led them to the room on the right. Esther paused in the doorway. The colour scheme was off white and cream, a pale brown lounge suite scattered in the middle of the room around a rustic coffee table. Neither the furniture nor the floor to ceiling built-in bookcase, with glass doors, held her attention.

A young man rose to his feet, his dark eyes fixed on Esther. He had close cropped dark hair, an angular face with slashing cheeks, a row of earrings up both ears and in one eyebrow, and broad shoulders. "You have them with you." He gestured towards her handbag. A black feather was tattooed on his left palm.

She had the urge to place her hand against the handbag, as if to protect the contents from him. "How do you know?"

Jesse smiled slightly. "People don't always appreciate the truth."

"He used to be a demon," Malachi said.

Esther stepped back, spinning when she collided with someone. She felt warmth fill her cheeks when she realised she'd run into Malachi's gran. The woman's face was lined and full of hollows, her grey hair pulled back into a plait that ended past her shoulders. After a glance at Esther, her hazel eyes focused on Malachi.

"Your parents are concerned about you, Malachi." Gran offered her cheek to him for a kiss.

He kissed her cheek. "They always are."

"Should they be?"

Esther was surprised at how strong the elderly woman's voice was, her initial thoughts of fleeing having momentarily vanished at her appearance. They returned again, not as urgent this time.

Malachi chuckled. "No more than usual."

Gran inclined her head. "I'll make sure to mention you in my evening prayers."

Those words had Esther wanting to flee again. She'd had more than enough to do with religion.

"Something about that bothers you," Jesse said.

Esther turned to see he watched her carefully. She shrugged. "I've lived with religious people before." She faced Malachi. "Is this your answer? Because praying didn't help earlier, only the daggers."

Jesse held out a hand, the one without the feather tattoo. "Can I see them?"

This time Esther did place her hand protectively over her handbag. "What do you know about them?"

Gran strode further into the room. "Everyone take

a seat. We need to know what is going on before we can offer any advice."

Esther found herself obeying the commanding voice, wanting to rise from the seat as soon as she'd sat down. It took her a moment to control the urge. She had no idea what to do. Trying to start over again obviously didn't work for her. Yet neither had her old life been working out.

Malachi sat on the large, square footstool in front of the armchair Esther sat on, drawing it to the side first. "Esther found a book detailing what Elvera is doing to her."

"Show me," Gran said.

When Esther remained still, Malachi placed a hand over hers that remained pressed against the handbag. "They can help. I wouldn't have brought you here if I didn't think they could help. This is what my family do. Save people from demons."

Esther's gaze was drawn to Jesse. "How does that work when you are a demon?"

"Demons are like humans. There are both good and evil amongst them." Jesse smiled again. "And I am no longer a demon."

Esther wasn't sure she believed him. Not with how he knew she carried the daggers.

"Esther." Malachi's voice was soft.

She turned her gaze from Jesse to Malachi. His hand remained over hers and she saw something in his eyes that she didn't immediately recognise. He was worried about her. Panic rushed through her. Why did he care what happened? What was she meant to do about that? She opened her mouth to speak, closing it again. How had her life reached the point where it scared her when someone actually cared? When had it become a strange occurrence? She slipped her hand out from beneath his, taking the book out once he shifted his hand. She held it out to Jesse.

"I will-" Jesse started to take the book, drawing back when his fingers touched the cover. "It has been bound in human flesh. A sacrificed human."

Esther dropped the book as if she'd been stung, staring at it on the floor at her feet. She wanted to ask him if she'd heard correctly, but from the distasteful look on Scarlett's face, she assumed she had. "What does that mean?"

"Could it have been the book you sensed and not the daggers?" Scarlett asked.

Jesse's gaze remained on the book. "Anything is possible, Lady Knight."

"Show them the daggers," Malachi said.

Leaving the book on the floor, Esther took out

the three timber boxes, setting them on her lap. She opened one, holding out the dagger on her palm, the blade and the hilt extending beyond the length of her hand.

"There are three of them?" Jesse asked.

Esther nodded, but didn't open the other two boxes. "All identical."

Jesse looked from the dagger to the book and back again. "If that book is what I think it is, it will explain in great detail about the executioner daggers. As well as many other things best not tampered with."

"What is it?" Esther asked.

"Once people thought they were a witch's grimoire. They were partly wrong. They belong to a demon, not a witch, and the rituals typically have an injurious or destructive purpose," Jesse said.

"A book of spells?" Esther's gaze was drawn to the book.

"No, a book of invocations and rituals. Demonic rituals."

"Should we burn it?" Scarlett asked.

Esther snatched it off the floor, trying not to think about what the cover was made from. "I need it. There's information in it I need to learn."

"We will not burn it," Gran said. "Knowledge is

never bad. It is what one chooses to do with that knowledge that is good or bad."

Malachi rose to his feet. "If all the information is in the grimoire, we should leave before Elvera finds us."

"Sit down, child. No need to rush off." Gran gestured towards the footstool, the long sleeve of her blouse drawing back from her wrist to show the start of her demon mark.

"Gran–"

Gran interrupted Malachi. "There's no need to go rushing after danger. It will find you soon enough."

"That's what I'm worried about," Malachi muttered as he sat on the footstool.

"Will the daggers hurt us?" Esther returned the book to her handbag, preferring not to touch the cover any longer than necessary. She put the daggers away too.

"Depends on what you consider harm." Jesse crossed the space between them unnaturally fast, clasping her arms to turn her wrists upwards. "An executioner is different from a hunter. You might want to learn what that entails before you use the daggers again."

Chapter Sixteen

Esther started to pull away from Jesse, ignoring Scarlett's protests that he shouldn't push himself like that. She froze, her gaze caught by what looked like a dried spot of blood at each pulse point. "What-" She broke off, not sure she wanted her question answered.

"Each time you sever all a demon's ties to existence, you take a little piece of their power for yourself. Possibly corrupted power that will, in turn, corrupt you." Jesse let go of her arms.

Esther continued to hold them up, her gaze fixed on the marks. "I don't feel any different."

"One minor demon won't make a noticeable difference." Jesse shrugged. "It could take five, or ten, or only a single demon more powerful than you expected."

"When did I get the marks?" Esther met Jesse's gaze, finally able to draw her own from the marks.

"You would have felt them," Jesse said. "The pain isn't easily forgotten. Or so I've been told."

Her breath caught in her throat. The sharp sensation she'd felt after executing Torrnon? He was right. It wouldn't be easily forgotten.

"What should they do with them?" Scarlett asked.

Jesse shrugged again. "That will depend on what outcome Esther is looking for."

Esther wanted to run. Wanted to leave the book and daggers behind and run as far and fast as possible. An image of her blood dripping into a wine glass filled her mind. Running wouldn't help. She met Jesse's gaze. "What am I meant to do? Let Elvera steal my body? Die so she can take it over?"

Malachi took hold of Esther's hand, drawing it closer to him, clasping it tight. "I will not allow that to happen."

Gran rose to her feet. "The two of you need to leave. I can have someone meet you later in the night and take over the driving for you."

"We have to-" Esther stared up at the elderly woman. "Why-" She tried to think of a question that didn't sound like a demand. Why were they being thrown out?

Malachi, still holding Esther's hand, drew her to her

feet. "We'll wait to hear from you if you come up with any ideas."

Scarlett also rose to her feet, throwing her arms around Malachi. "Don't go rushing into danger. Give us a chance to figure something out."

Malachi grinned. "You want me to break the habit of a lifetime?"

Scarlett smiled at him. "Yes." Her smile faded as she turned to Esther. "Don't feel like we're kicking you out. Gran sometimes gives orders rather than explanations."

"There is no need to apologise for me, child." Gran looked Esther up and down. "The girl is stronger than she appears. She's weathered more than her fair share of bad storms."

Esther felt her cheeks warm again, not knowing if she should thank Gran or remain silent. She went with the second option, starting to turn away when Malachi tugged her towards the door.

"Esther." Jesse stepped forward, waiting for her to meet his gaze before he continued talking. "You need all three daggers nearby and two must break the skin, one causing a mortal wound, for them to work. The demon also needs to be bound to the executioner in some way. Having the demon consume your blood is usually the easiest."

Esther held his gaze, ideas rushing through her mind, none of them fully formed. "Bound, such as for an extrication?"

Jesse nodded. "The longer a demon has lived on this earth, the more powerful they will be. Being as this demon wears the skin of a human, it will allow them to walk the earth day or night regardless of their level of power."

"Her," Esther said. "Elvera."

"That won't be her name. She would have taken the name along with the skin of her previous victim," Jesse said.

"How would I find out-" Esther broke off as she realised Elvera's name. Her demon name. "Dazreyella."

"Are you certain?" Jesse demanded.

"You know her?" Scarlett slipped an arm around Jesse's waist. "Would she know you? Is it safe for you to be involved in going after her?"

Jesse shook his head. "I only know of her."

"So do I," Gran said.

Esther didn't like the tone of voice both of them used. It gave her an ominous feeling. "Who is she? Some sort of demon celebrity?"

"You need to leave. Dazreyella would not be above

using humans to enter this house." Gran ushered them to the front door.

"I need to kn–"

Gran interrupted Esther. "I will call you and Malachi later and you can ask your questions then. For now, you need to leave. You aren't as safe here as I thought you'd be."

A sense of urgency rushed through Esther and she grabbed her shoes, pulling them on. "She might be outside?"

"I'll check for you." Jesse opened the door and strode outside, Scarlett following and protesting that he wasn't to leave her behind.

Finished putting on her shoes, Esther turned to Gran. "Thank you." She wasn't sure how any of them could help, but she was beginning to think they were sincere in their offer to help her escape Elvera's plans.

Gran momentarily rested a hand on Esther's shoulder. "Go with God."

She wanted to protest that she didn't exactly believe in him. That she hadn't since that night so many years ago. Somehow, she managed not to blurt out the words that had first come to mind and thanked Gran once more before stepping outside, Malachi following her.

She scanned the area, surprisingly reassured to see

Jesse and Scarlett doing the same, the lights at the front of the house enough to show nothing was lurking nearby. Reaching the vehicle, she started to open the door.

Jesse glanced at them before continuing to scan the area. "I checked the vehicle. It hasn't been tampered with."

Esther lowered her hand, not having considered that possibility.

Jesse glanced at her again. "That was reassurance, not a warning."

Scarlett chuckled. "Considering how long you've lived, you'd think you'd be better at making sure people can tell which one you're offering."

Esther began to ask how long Jesse had been alive, deciding there were probably some things she was better off not knowing. Opening the vehicle door, she clambered in, wishing she didn't need to spend more hours stuck in the vehicle. She wanted this to be over so she could figure out what she was going to do with her life. This new start had obviously not worked out in the least. She had to come up with a better plan.

It was too dark to read 'Demonology' and she found herself playing with the phone Elvera had given her. It was still off.

Malachi glanced at her. "What are you thinking of doing?"

She stared at the phone, the splashes of light from the streetlights they passed regularly highlighting it. "I should get rid of it. Before I ring and tell her there's no way I'm going to let her take over my body."

"That might be a good plan. Annoying her could either make the situation worse or have her accidentally reveal her plans." Malachi chuckled. "From experience, there's usually about a fifty percent chance it'll help."

Her gaze was drawn to Malachi. "You deliberately annoy people."

He chuckled again. "Occasionally. Sometimes it occurs naturally."

Her lips reluctantly curved into a smile. "Now that I can believe."

Malachi slowed for the red light ahead of them. "You going to call her?"

She ran her thumb over the screen of the phone. "I don't know." She frowned. Being more cautious obviously wasn't working out for her. She turned on the phone. "Yeah, I think I am."

"Don't leave the phone on too long. She might be able to use it to track where you are." Malachi stopped behind the other vehicles waiting for the red light.

The moment the phone was on, Esther dialled Elvera's number, ignoring all the notifications from messages and missed calls.

The phone barely had the chance to ring before it was answered. "Return to my house immediately and I will not come after all those you know. Both family and friends."

Esther hesitated a moment. With the tone Elvera had used, she didn't doubt the woman would do exactly as she threatened. "I have no one." Or at least no one that Elvera should know about. Her last foster parents hadn't believed in social media so even her online footprint was non-existent.

"Norman will find someone you care about."

"I've been a foster kid most of my life. There is no one. Do you think I'd have ended up in the system if there had been someone to take me in?"

"There is the demon hunter. Norman said he came to the house twice. That sounds like someone you might miss having around," Elvera said.

Esther hesitated. She forced herself to relax. There was no way Elvera could know how she felt about Malachi. Particularly since she didn't exactly know. "Oh, him. He just turned up at the right time to check there weren't any more demons. It surprised me."

"I could kill him and it wouldn't bother you," Elvera stated.

"Not at all," Esther said breezily. "He's nothing to me." When Malachi glanced at her, she mouthed the word sorry, hoping there was enough light filtering into the vehicle for him to see.

"It doesn't matter. I will find you. There's nowhere you can hide that I will not eventually find you. Your days on this earth are limited. You had best make the most of them."

Before Esther could reply, Malachi took the phone from her and turned it off. She started to protest then remembered she was supposed to be limiting the amount of time the phone was on. "You know I didn't mean what I said about you, don't you?"

"It would be understandable if you did." Malachi glanced at her. "You don't really know me."

She rested her hand on his arm. "I do know you and I'd hate for anything to happen to you."

He took a hand off the steering wheel to place it over hers for a moment. "I wouldn't want anything to happen to you either."

Esther tried to think of something to break the silence which now seemed awkward. "I want to go after her. I don't want to sit around waiting for her to come for me. That's not who I am. If someone picks a fight with me, I face them head on."

"That sounds like my kind of plan, but this time it might not be a good idea. You don't have the experience to face demons and survive."

"I might not have much experience of demons, but I've got enough experience at fighting." According to her last foster parents, she had too much experience at fighting.

Malachi laughed softly. "We'll come up with a plan you can be involved in."

"Good." Silence descended between them again, but this time Esther didn't find it uncomfortable. She looked out the window at the traffic ahead of them, the vehicle not having moved since they came to a stop at the red light. "The light is green. Why aren't we moving?"

Malachi handed over his phone. "Check the road conditions."

It didn't take her long to discover a major accident had brought traffic to a halt. She relayed the details to Malachi. "What are we going to do?" Looking out the windows she saw they were surrounded by other vehicles. It was impossible to move.

"If we're stuck here too long, you might have to

leave without me. You're the only one they can track. You and possibly the daggers."

She wanted to protest, but the shock of realising she'd been about to protest because she didn't want to leave, kept her silent. It wasn't like she was incapable of looking after herself. She was more than capable. Had taken care of herself for years. "Okay. Where will we meet if we get separated?"

"Ring me. We can figure out where's the closest place," Malachi said.

"What if one or both of us lose our phone?" Esther asked.

"Then we'll meet at my place. If you can find your way back there," Malachi said.

She thought over the directions they'd taken. "Yeah. That'll work."

Malachi didn't speak immediately. "You should probably go."

Again she wanted to protest. "I suppose." She reached for the door.

He wrapped his hand around her wrist, drawing her back from the door. "Be careful."

Chapter Seventeen

Esther met Malachi's gaze, surprised at his expression. Not knowing what to say, she nodded before slipping from his grasp and opening the door. Closing the door behind her, she darted through the stationary traffic. She ignored the urge to check over her shoulder. She'd only known him for a few days. He shouldn't be that important to her. It shouldn't bother her to leave him behind.

Reaching the footpath, she glanced around, trying to decide which direction to take. She supposed it didn't really matter. She continued to walk in the direction they'd been going before taking the next left. There was no way she wanted to get anywhere near the accident. Not while she carried three daggers. The area was probably filled with cops and she didn't want to risk any of them searching her handbag. She couldn't imagine that would go down all that well particularly with the book she carried.

She continued along the streets, taking random turns, fighting the urge to look over her shoulder. That would slow her down. When she did eventually look over her shoulder, it was to find that she didn't have a clue if anyone was following her. Even with all the streetlights that allowed her to clearly see those striding along the footpath with her. A couple of times she checked her phone. There were no messages or missed calls from Malachi. How long would it take him to get out of the backed up traffic and onto less congested roads? Wandering around the streets alone made her feel like she had a target on her back. One that everyone could see.

When Malachi did ring, she had somehow wandered away from the main streets and was amongst industrial buildings, wondering if she should bring up the local map on her phone in an effort to help her find her way to a more populated area. Continuing in the direction she'd been going, she answered the phone. "Where are you?"

"I was about to ask the same."

She grinned at Malachi's reply. "I have no idea. Some industrial estate by the look of it." Reaching an intersection, she read out the street names to him.

"How did you end up there?"

"It was because you took so long."

"I won't be much longer. I'm about fifteen minutes away from you."

"Good. I'm tired. When is your gran going to ring?"

"She already has."

She'd wanted to be there to ask questions and find out what was going on. "What did she say?"

"I'll tell you when I pick you up. See you soon."

"Okay." When she ended the call, the silence pressed in on her. She scanned the area. Nothing moved. She was alone. Yet it didn't feel like that. It felt like someone watched her. She pressed a hand against her handbag. If someone was hoping to mug her, she couldn't afford to lose the daggers. They might be her only chance to beat Elvera.

By the time Malachi arrived, she was jumping at every sound. She hurried towards him, glancing over her shoulder as she got in the vehicle. "That must've been the longest fifteen minutes ever." She buckled up as he drove off.

"Did something happen?"

She shook her head. "What did your gran have to say?"

Malachi glanced at her a couple of times before he

spoke. "She has some of our family looking into the possibility of breaking your connection to Elvera."

"Why aren't you figuring out ways to kill her? I thought you were meant to be demon hunters."

Malachi laughed softly. "We are. The priority is to keep you safe. Then find a way of taking Elvera down."

"Isn't it better to leave her bound to me so she doesn't go after someone else?" Not that she liked the idea of Elvera hunting her.

"If we break the bond between you, we won't have to remain on the move. It'll give us a better chance to figure out what to do next," Malachi said.

"I don't think it'll help that much. What we need is some way of knowing where Elvera is. How can we track her down?"

"That sounds like a dangerous idea."

She examined him in the limited light. "From what your family have said, I would have thought that was exactly your kind of idea."

He remained silent for a moment before glancing at her. "They worry too much. I have the skills and knowledge to deal with the situations I get myself into."

"Why don't you just come straight out and say that I don't?" Esther demanded.

"I'm sure you don't need me telling you something you already know."

She opened her mouth to argue further, closing it instead of speaking. She stared out the window. "Sorry. I know you're trying to help." She turned towards him again. "If you knew me better, you'd know I don't run."

"Sometimes it's necessary."

"We need to come up with a better plan. Because running isn't necessary." She looked out the window again. It didn't matter what he said, she wasn't about to run. Never again. The sound of crackling flames filled her mind. She pushed them away. It was the last thing she wanted to think about tonight. It was bad enough the memories interrupted when she wasn't in danger.

Malachi pulled up behind a parked four-wheel-drive. "I actually feel a little bit of sympathy for my family right now." He grinned. "Only a little bit. It wouldn't be so bad if you had the skills to face demons." He turned off the engine.

"Then you better teach me." She scanned the area. "What are we doing?"

"Having a sleep. Bring all the gear you need. Do you want me to open the boot?"

"We're leaving your car here?" She didn't have

much, but all she owned was in the vehicle, most of it in the boot. She didn't want to risk losing what little she had.

"No. Scarlett will take it to my place while Jesse drives us around while we sleep in the back seat." Malachi opened the door, pausing before he got out. "If you need something later, we can always call into my place and pick it up."

"Okay. There's nothing I need to take with me other than my handbag and the book you let me borrow." She picked up the book, not putting it in her already cluttered handbag, and followed him to the parked vehicle.

Once they were both seated and buckled up, Jesse drove off, leaving Scarlett behind. He glanced over his shoulder. "There's an esky behind the seat with sandwiches if you're hungry. Ryan's idea."

"Thanks." Malachi reached over the back of the seat and picked up the small esky, sharing out the sandwiches.

"Who is Ryan?" Esther asked.

"Another one of my cousins." Malachi had a bite of his sandwich.

"How many cousins do you have?" Esther lifted up a corner of the bread to check what was on the sandwich.

Jesse chuckled. "I think their family took the bible verse of 'be fruitful and multiply' rather seriously."

Seeing the sandwich was roast beef and salad, Esther let go of the edge of the bread. "There are a lot of you?" She took a bite.

"We're scattered around the country. And the world," Malachi said. "Not all of them are first cousins."

When they remained silent for a bit, Jesse spoke. "Was there anywhere in particular you wanted to go?"

"After Elvera," Esther muttered.

"I take it you didn't read up on the daggers," Jesse said.

"Why do you say that?" Esther had the last mouthful of her sandwich.

"Have a look. There's a torch in the back pocket of the front passenger seat," Jesse said.

She found the torch and used it to search through the book. "I can't find anything about executioner daggers." She'd found a lot of other things that looked interesting. Things she planned to read about later.

"What about carnifex pugione?" Jesse asked.

Malachi, who'd been leaning close as Esther glanced through the pages, reached for the book. "I remember seeing that."

"What does it mean?" Esther handed over the book.

"It's Latin," Jesse said. "Executioner dagger."

"Here." Malachi pointed to the title of the page. He ran his finger down the page. "Good thing the rest of it isn't in Latin. Mine is extremely rusty."

"I would have been able to translate it for you." Jesse slowed for a red light.

Esther checked out the window, thoughts of the other red light coming to mind. The traffic was light and she doubted there was another accident to hold them up.

"I see why you suggested reading it," Malachi said.

Esther looked to where he pointed, excitement rushing through her as she read the words. "I can hunt down Nethod. I got his blood on one of the daggers. Maybe he'll be able to tell us where Elvera is."

"We need a map." Malachi handed the book to Esther. "I doubt pulling up a map on my phone would work."

"It might," Jesse said. "It is a map. Although I don't know how the blood will form on the location or if it would damage your phone. It fades after awhile on paper."

"Where will we find a map?" Esther turned off the

torch and closed the book. She'd read more about the daggers later. After she found out where Nethod was.

"Service stations sometimes sell them." Jesse slowed for a corner. "I can see one further along this road." He glanced over his shoulder. "There's always the chance Elvera might have bled on one of the daggers. It doesn't matter which dagger the blood marks or which dagger you use to search for the demon. Until their ties to all existence are severed, they can always be tracked down by using the daggers."

Esther frowned. "You keep wording it like that. Why don't you just say until they're dead?'

"Demons don't die in the sense that humans do. They cease to exist. Depending on how they cease to exist, there is a chance in the future that they might exist again. Not those who have ceased to exist by use of the executioner daggers though."

When they pulled up at the service station, Malachi hopped out, telling Esther to wait for him in the vehicle. If demons turned up in the area, they'd need to leave quickly. She watched him stride towards the service station, tense as she waited for his return. She half expected something to go wrong and was surprised when it didn't. She shifted back over when he clambered in the vehicle, bringing several folded maps.

Esther took them from Malachi before he buckled up. "They're local maps?"

"One of Australia, one of Queensland and one of Brisbane." Finished buckling up, Malachi reached for one of the maps, unfolding it. "I thought we could start with the Brisbane one and if we have no luck you can try the Queensland map then the Australian one. We don't know if she's remained nearby. She could have left the country for all we know."

Jesse pulled out onto the road. "We won't be able to do the ritual in the back seat. Why don't you both get some sleep while Scarlett organises everything you need. Send her a photo of the page so she knows what needs to be done."

Esther was tempted to protest. She wanted to find out where Elvera was right now.

Malachi took out his phone. "Can you open the book up to the page about the daggers?"

Esther found the page, holding it open. "How long will it take? What if Elvera's in Brisbane, but planning to leave shortly? We might miss her."

Malachi took a photo of the page and sent it. "I told Scarlett it's urgent. To do it as quickly as possible."

Esther's reply was interrupted by a message coming through on Malachi's phone. "Is that her? What did she say?"

Malachi looked up from the screen of his phone. "She asked if we're certain we wish to do this."

Esther didn't hesitate. "Of course I am. I'm not about to spend the rest of my life running."

Nodding, Malachi sent a message. He put his phone away. "We should get some sleep. It's after midnight." He grinned at her. "Want to use my shoulder as a pillow?"

"There are a couple of pillows in the back, behind your seats," Jessie said.

"Thanks," Malachi said dryly.

Jesse chuckled. "Any time."

Malachi reached over the back of the seat and brought forward two pillows. He handed one to Esther.

She glanced at his shoulder before taking it. She wasn't sure if she was disappointed he'd been unable to follow through on his offer. "Thank you."

Malachi grinned. "The offer of a shoulder is still there if you want it."

Again her gaze was drawn to his shoulder. The offer was surprisingly tempting. "Maybe another day."

Malachi leaned closer, lowering his voice before he spoke. "I'll hold you to that."

She stared at him in the semidarkness, regular

splashes of light clearly showing his expression. It didn't help, she had no idea what he was thinking. Rather than worry about it, she made herself comfortable, leaning against the pillow once it was in place.

Chapter Eighteen

Esther hadn't expected to fall asleep, but she found herself being woken by the early morning light. She remained still, taking in her surroundings, her gaze scanning Malachi's features. He'd turned towards her in his sleep, his lips slowly curving into a smile. Obviously, his dreams tended to be better than hers. As she watched, his eyes slowly opened.

He blinked twice before his smile fully formed. "Morning."

She straightened, glancing away. "I thought Scarlett was going to ring us."

Jesse glanced over his shoulder, currently stopped at a red light. "She messaged me earlier. Neither of you stirred in your sleep so I let you be."

"I need to deal–"

Jesse interrupted Esther. "You need to be well rested when you deal with demons. Your hours of sleep might make the difference between success and failure."

She opened her mouth to argue, closing it when Malachi took hold of her hand, cradling it between his.

"You can trust Jesse. He knows a lot about demons."

"In this matter, you can trust me," Jesse corrected.

Esther stared at the back of Jesse's head, not sure that she wanted to know which matters she couldn't trust him in. "Can we use the daggers to find Nethod now?"

"I'm currently heading to Malachi's place with a slight detour on the way for breakfast." Jesse glanced at them over his shoulder. "Any requests?"

Esther shrugged. "I don't care. Something fast and easy so we can get on with being the ones doing the tracking. I'm sick of it being the other way around."

Jesse took them through the drive-through at the next fast food shop they saw. Twenty minutes later, food eaten, they were pulling up at Malachi's house. Scarlett opened the front door as they clambered out of the vehicle.

Esther looked at Malachi, who she walked beside, Jesse having gone ahead of them. "Your cousin has a key to your house?"

"Gran has a key to my house. Scarlett would have collected it."

Esther looked between Scarlett, who was greeting Jesse, her arms wrapped around him, and Malachi. She couldn't imagine trusting her cousins with the key to anywhere she lived. She doubted there was much of anything she could trust her cousins with. "You and your family are close." She'd meant it as a statement, but it came out sounding more like a question.

"I trust my family with my life and have done many times."

She came to a stop, staring up at him. What would that be like? Then she realised. She already knew. Her parents had saved her life that night, sending her ahead of them even though they couldn't follow. "That isn't always a good thing."

He didn't answer immediately. "Not everyone understands that."

"You two coming inside? You can't stay in one place too long," Scarlett reminded them.

Esther strode inside, coming to a halt when she saw the five candles set up on the table along with matches, a shallow metal bowl and dried herbs. Fear arrowed through her. "Is this safe?" She made a vague gesture with her hand. "I mean, none of you will be hurt from this?"

"There are different types of hurts," Jessie said.

"That is such a demon answer," Malachi said. "How about a straight one for a change?"

Jesse met Malachi's gaze. "I would not allow Scarlett to help if she would come to physical harm from participating." His lips curved into a smile as he glanced at Scarlett. "Her soul, now that is her concern."

Scarlett came closer, stopping directly in front of Esther. "Didn't Jessie explain to you the dangers of meddling with things related to demons?"

Esther shook her head. "What sort of dangers?"

"The sort that endangers your soul. He should have warned you." Scarlett gave Jesse a look, that he answered with a shrug and a half smile.

When Scarlett continued to look at him, Jesse asked, "Lady Knight, would you make me responsible for the souls of all those I come into contact with?"

Scarlett sighed. "No, of course not." She turned to Esther. "Some things can endanger your soul and ensure you end up in hell. Think carefully before you follow any instructions from the demon grimoire. It could come with a heavier price than you expect."

She didn't need to think it over. She'd worry about

her soul later. If she managed to live long enough to worry about it. Right now, she was more concerned with her physical well being. "This is everything that was in the book?"

Scarlett nodded, capturing Esther's arm when she started to walk past. "What we know is that demon executioners were once a good thing. Either a human or demon who ensured that any demon who became out of control was dealt with. Permanently."

Esther tugged her arm from Scarlett's light grip. "I only plan to use the daggers to track down two demons. After that, I won't need to use them again." She took the boxes from her handbag and set them on the table, placing the grimoire beside them.

Jesse put a hand over one of the boxes when Esther tried to open it. "The daggers might have other plans for you should you use them more than once or twice."

The memory of driving the dagger into Torrnon came to mind. It had been an oddly satisfying moment. "I could think of worse things."

Jesse inclined his head, moving his hand out of the way. "So could I."

Esther opened the book, glancing at Malachi when he came to stand beside her. She read over the instructions, frowning at times as she struggled to decipher the script the words had been written in. After placing each of the daggers by three separate candles, she put the metal bowl in front of the candle closest to her. Next, she lit the candles then crumbled the herbs into the bowl and set them alight too. Picking up one of the daggers, she ran it through the smoke from the herbs before nicking her arm with the tip of the blade.

Blood welled up, seeming to soak into the blade. A shiver ran through her at the impossibility of the moment. She almost stopped. Nearly put the daggers away and blew out the candles. Straightening her shoulders, she took the map from Malachi and placed it in the middle of the table. She wasn't about to let Elvera win. Losing would mean death and she wasn't ready to die.

Holding the dagger over the map, she stared at the paper. Her gaze was drawn to the few locations she knew. She started to lower the dagger, wondering if she'd done something wrong. Three spots of blood began to form, darkening the map in three separate locations.

"How do I know who they are?" Esther lowered the dagger, keeping hold of it.

"You don't. All the daggers care about is that those demons have been marked by one of them," Jesse said. "They may have been accidentally marked and should not have all ties severed to existence."

Frustration raced through her. "What am I meant to do?"

"Go after them and see what they are doing," Malachi said. "I'll go with you."

"What if none of them are Nethod or Elvera?" Esther asked.

"Then we look further afield." Malachi took the dagger from her, returning it to the box. "Which one do you want to go after first? We can't stay here any longer without the risk of being caught."

She started to point to one of the blood spots, freezing when she saw one of the other ones was moving slowly across the map. "Is it meant to do that?"

"You're tracking demons. They don't stay in one place unless they're busy doing something there. Not always something innocent," Jesse said.

She stared at the blood spot as it moved across the map. "We'll follow that one."

Malachi blew out the candles. "We can clean this mess up later." He led the way to the vehicle, Jesse and Scarlett following. "Want me to drive?"

Jesse shook his head. "We're meeting up with

Blake. He'll take over so Scarlett and I can have a sleep."

Malachi opened the back passenger door. "Allie won't be with him?"

Scarlett clambered in the front passenger seat. "No, much to her disappointment. Problems with her parents again."

"I have a feeling she won't be staying at home much longer." Jesse started the vehicle, reversing out onto the road once everyone was seated.

Esther stared at the blood spot. It continued to move. She gave directions as it made its way across Brisbane, heading towards the Gold Coast. After an hour, she looked out the window when they pulled up on the side of the road. "What are we doing?"

Jesse gestured towards the four-wheel-drive parked in front of them. "Time for a new chauffeur."

Malachi leaned forward, clasping hand to arm first with Scarlett and then Jesse, the starting point of their demon marks making contact. "Thanks."

"Be careful." Scarlett looked from Malachi to Esther, smiling. "Both of you." She looked at Malachi again. "I'll let you know if we learn anything new."

"I can only tell you about it from the perspective of one who is being hunted," Jesse said.

Scarlett placed her hand on his forearm. "You were hunted by an executioner?"

"No, a brother was. He was wrongly hunted."

"I'm sorry." Scarlett's words were soft.

Esther turned away from the look they gave each other, feeling like she was intruding on the moment. Clambering out of the vehicle, she said a quiet goodbye over her shoulder before closing the door and following Malachi to the next vehicle. She glanced at the map she carried. The blood spot had moved further away. She waited until she was seated in the back, and greetings were done, before she spoke. "How are we meant to catch him? He keeps staying one step ahead."

"We might be trying to track the wrong one," Malachi said.

Blake turned in his seat so he could meet Esther's gaze. "Where to?"

She sighed, tilting the map so he could see where they were going. "If he goes too much further, I'll need another map."

Malachi took out his phone as Blake drove off. He typed in a message, putting his phone away once he received a reply. "If you need a new map, you'll need to do the ritual again."

"Did you want to track down one of the other demons?" Blake asked.

Her grip tightened on the map. She bit back the words she started to say. Ones of anger and frustration. "Everything can be picked up in a supermarket. If he goes off the map, we can call into one and I can get the items I need to use on a new map."

"We can't stay anywhere for very long," Malachi said.

She unfolded the map, trying not to crumple the large piece of paper too much. "The other demons are still in the same locations they were in earlier."

"If one of them is Elvera, she could be sending humans out to track you down. Or other demons who haven't been marked by the daggers," Malachi said.

"What's the verdict?" Blake asked. "Keep following or turn back?"

Esther didn't hesitate. She wasn't about to let the demon get away. "Keep following him. But call into the next supermarket you see. We need to get supplies and a map for the area he's going towards."

"I can see a shopping centre ahead of us that has a couple of supermarkets. Will it do?" Blake asked.

Esther shrugged. "I don't know. Are the supermarkets easily accessed?"

Malachi took out his phone. "There's one not far from one of the entrances."

"It will do." Esther folded the map, needing to refold it a couple of times when the paper didn't cooperate.

Malachi directed Blake to the correct entrance and they found a park not far from it. Once they were out of the vehicle, Blake leaned close to Esther. "If we're separated, there's a spare key in a magnetic box under the front of the vehicle."

A shiver ran through her and she pressed her hand against her handbag, feeling the various hard shapes inside it. "Why would we be separated?"

"We shouldn't," Blake said. "I just want to make sure you have a way to get out of here fast if we do. You're the one the demons are after." He nodded towards the shopping centre entrance. "Ready?"

Nodding, she strode towards the entrance, trying not to think about needing to spend money she really couldn't afford to waste. Who knew how long it was going to take to deal with Elvera and she could return to looking for work. The money Norman had given her and the little amount in her bank account wouldn't last long with the cost of living. Nor would the hundred dollar notes she'd taken from the safe. As she stepped inside the shopping centre, she took out her phone to check her bank balance. She knew it was under a hundred dollars, but wanted an exact amount.

She came to a stop, staring at the screen of her phone, refreshing the page to make sure there was no mistake.

Malachi returned to her side. "What's wrong?"

"I was paid."

Malachi frowned. "Paid for what?"

She met his gaze. "Elvera paid me. I'm meant to be paid every Tuesday." She turned the phone to show him the figure. "I was paid this morning. For the work I've done for Elvera. Every cent she said I'd be paid."

"She probably set up automatic payments." Blake gestured towards the supermarket ahead of them. "We have to keep moving."

Chapter Nineteen

Dazed, Esther nodded and hurried after Blake, logging out of her bank account and slipping her phone into her handbag. The image of her bank account balance went round in her head. Why hadn't Elvera cancelled the payment? Would she demand the money back?

Malachi slipped his hand in hers, squeezing lightly before letting go. "It will be okay."

She nearly asked him how he could say that. Pushing the question away, she nodded instead. Surely one time things had to work out for her. Who knew. This might be that one time.

It didn't take long to gather the items they needed and they headed to the checkout. Blake waved Esther's money aside, paying for everything. He grabbed the bag and strode towards the exit.

Esther hurried after him. "I didn't need you to pay for it."

Blake didn't slow his pace. "You don't know how long you'll be unable to work."

"What about you? How are you meant to work when you're helping me?" Esther asked.

Blake chuckled, glancing at her. "I am working."

Before Esther could comment, a security guard stepped in front of her. "Come with me Ms."

Esther took a step back from the security guard who loomed over her. "What for?"

"If you will come this way please." He gestured in the opposite direction to what they'd been taking.

"You don't have to go with him," Blake said. "He isn't a police officer. If he wants you to go somewhere, he'll have to call the police and have them take you there. If they think the situation warrants it."

Malachi slipped an arm around her shoulders, his gaze on the security guard. "What is this about?"

"You two are free to go. It is only the young woman who needs to come with me," the security guard said.

"You never told me why." Esther glared at him. "I'm not going with you unless I know why."

"I can call the police if you force me to, but I would

think you'd prefer to resolve this matter quietly," the security guard said.

"You never explained what the matter is," Malachi said.

Blake, who'd been staring at the screen of his phone, looked up from it. "We should have checked this shopping centre out before we stopped here. Guess whose company owns it."

"Elvera." Esther's hands tightened into fists. She wasn't about to go anywhere with the security guard.

"If you refuse to cooperate, I will call the police." The security guard took out a phone.

"Give me a minute to say goodbye." She couldn't risk that he wasn't bluffing. Facing Malachi, she reached up a hand to press it against his cheek, rising onto the tip of her toes. Her lips were close enough to feel the warmth of his breath caressing her. "Don't let her get the daggers and book." She shielded her handbag with her body, pressing it into Malachi's hand.

His other hand slid around the back of her head, keeping her close, his fingers splayed through her hair, his gaze colliding with hers. "Don't go with him."

"What if he calls the cops? I can't lose the daggers." They might be her only means of beating Elvera.

"I'll meet you at your place." She tried to smile reassuringly, lowering her hand to slip the strap of her handbag down her arm. "Go." She turned him from her, trying to keep the security guard from seeing that Malachi had her handbag.

"Esther–"

She interrupted Blake, continuing to keep her back to the security guard. "It will be okay." She repeated Malachi's earlier words, wondering if now was the time to begin praying they were true. Especially since demons were involved.

Blake inclined his head. "We'll wait for you."

"Don't." She took a step back from Malachi. "Go." She waited until the two of them had joined the crowd heading away from her before she faced the security guard. "You can let Elvera know you have me."

"I have no idea what you are talking about." The security guard gestured in the same direction he'd indicated earlier. "This way."

She walked beside him, her gaze darting everywhere. Once she'd given Malachi and Blake enough time to leave, she was getting out of this place. They approached a corridor that had a sign indicating it led to centre management. She tensed. It was time to escape.

Norman strode out from the corridor, grabbing hold of Esther's shoulder before she could spin away. He met the security guard's gaze. "I will take it from here. Thank you."

The security guard nodded before heading back the way he'd come.

Esther stared after him, trying to ignore Norman's grip. His fingers dug into her shoulder, making it impossible to escape. Obviously, his blood wasn't on any of the daggers.

"Where are the items you took from her?" Norman headed down the corridor, his tight grip forcing her to remain at his side.

"I burned the book and sold the daggers so I could afford fuel. I didn't realise Elvera was going to pay me."

"I don't believe you." Norman's grip tightened on her.

She drew in a sharp breath. "Are you trying to break my shoulder?"

"I will break more than your shoulder if you don't tell me where everything is," Norman warned.

"I already told you. I don't have them anymore." She gritted her teeth at the pain in her shoulder. "If that is all this is about, you can let me go."

"You know that isn't all this is about. Elvera needs

you." He continued to drag her along the corridor, heading towards a lift.

"That's too bad." She tried to escape his grip. It was impossible and she gasped when his grip tightened further.

Norman forced her into the lift when it arrived, continuing to grip her shoulder. "Elvera will get the information out of you."

She stared at the numbers on the screen on the left. It was taking her below ground. Norman's grip remained tight on her shoulder. Her plans to escape looked like they weren't about to happen. After all she'd managed to escape it seemed wrong it would end like this. The crackle of flames filled her mind and she once again heard the screams. She wanted to run, but she was trapped in a small metal space with a demon.

The lift came to a stop and the doors slid open. Norman pushed her ahead of him, his grip remaining tight. "Don't try to run. Elvera would prefer the body unharmed, but she will accept whatever means I need to use to return you to her."

Her teeth remained clamped tight together, the ache in her shoulder growing worse by the minute. It was almost a relief when he shoved her in the back of his vehicle, firmly closing the door. She waited until he opened his door before she tested the handle. For a moment she thought she could escape. Panic swamped her when she realised it was child locked. Taking a deep breath, she pushed the panic away as she sank back against the seat. There had to be a way out of this mess.

As they came out from the underground parking, Esther peered out the window. The traffic was heavy and she eyed the window glass. It was unlikely she'd be able to break it and there was nothing for her to use. She'd have to see where he took her before she came up with a plan of escape.

When she saw their destination, she closed her eyes, tilting her head back against the seat. She'd already escaped Elvera's house once, surely she could do it again. Yet all she could think about was the wine Elvera gave her with dinner and the feeling of not being in control of her body when Elvera also inhabited it. There had to be a way to escape. She had to figure it out.

Norman swung the door open, this time not grabbing hold of her shoulder. "Inside. Don't keep Elvera waiting."

She nearly ran. Until she caught sight of Nethod glaring at her from beside the front door. There was no chance he'd let her escape. And he was likely to be rougher than Norman had been. Raising her chin, she strode towards the door when Norman gestured in that direction. She met Nethod's gaze as she passed him, tempted to tell him he'd be next. From the way his eyes narrowed, she assumed he heard the message clearly. Without her needing to voice it.

"You look terrible."

Esther's gaze was drawn from Nethod to Elvera who stood several metres inside the front door. Her jaw tightened. There were things she wanted to say to Elvera, just like with Nethod, but she doubted she'd need to voice them. The woman wasn't an idiot. She had to know Esther wasn't here willingly.

Elvera looked past Esther. "Put her in her room. I'll be there with the wine in a few minutes."

Esther watched Elvera stride towards the kitchen. She wanted to protest. Instead, she remained silent, her hands tightening into fists.

"Need a hand putting her in the room?" Nethod asked.

Not liking the tone of his voice, Esther started forward. "I know where it is." She heard footsteps behind her and hoped it was Norman. She didn't give any of them the satisfaction of checking. She stepped inside the room which had once seemed so amazing to her. Far too fancy for someone like her.

She supposed coffins were typically fancy. Again images came to mind, ones she couldn't focus on right now. She pushed them from her as she turned to face the doorway after stepping inside the room.

Norman remained in the doorway. He crossed his arms, staring at her, his expression neutral.

Elvera joined them, a glass of wine in her hands. It was filled to the brim. When Norman stepped out of the way she held it out to Esther. "Drink every drop."

Esther held her ground. "No."

Elvera continued to hold the glass out. "Shall I ask Nethod to make you drink it?"

Esther looked past Norman and Elvera to where Nethod stood well behind them, watching. As their gazes met, his lips twisted into a smile. She tried not to shudder. That smile clearly told her she wouldn't enjoy whatever means he came up with to make her drink the wine.

"Well?" Elvera demanded.

Esther took half a step forward, reaching out to take the wine glass. Meeting Elvera's gaze, she held it as she downed the contents that were more bitter than usual. She returned the glass. "You have no idea how to choose a nice wine."

"I will be back in half an hour." Elvera strode in the direction of the kitchen.

Norman closed the door, a clicking sound indicating it had been locked.

Even though she'd heard it lock, Esther had to check. It was exactly as she'd feared. There was no way through that door. She tried the window. It was locked too, the fancy bars unable to be unlatched. She breathed out heavily, spinning away from the window to stop when the bed caught her attention. She couldn't let Elvera take over her body. Already tiredness tugged at her.

She felt ill at the thought of Elvera using her like a puppet. Ill! She dashed to the bathroom, lifting the lid of the toilet and leaning over it as she tried to make herself throw up. It was harder than she'd expected, but eventually, she threw up the wine. Yet tiredness dragged at her. Flushing the toilet, she returned to the bedroom. Had she been too late?

She sat on the edge of the mattress, lowering her head into her hands. There had to be a way out of this. All Elvera needed to do was possess her three more times. She couldn't afford to let her possess her even a single time. Didn't dare risk it. Raising her head, she scanned the room. Nothing. Absolutely nothing that would help her escape.

She alternated between pacing and sitting on the edge of the mattress. A plan slowly formed, along with a smile. She glanced at the door before lying on the bed, her fingers lightly brushing over the cross at her throat. As long as she continued to wear a cross, Elvera wouldn't be able to possess her. She wouldn't have to do anything. Just lie here and wait for Elvera to discover she hadn't thrown it out.

She half drifted in and out of sleep as she waited for Elvera. The expected flash of pain eventually came. It took a great deal of effort to fake sleep when Elvera cursed her before striding from the room, calling for Norman to follow.

Chapter Twenty

Esther listened. She failed to hear the sound of the door closing. Keeping her eyes shut, she debated opening them to find out what was going on. Was she alone? She opened her eyes enough to look through her lashes. It didn't help. She could see nothing from where she lay. The sound of footsteps had her closing her eyes fully. She wanted to run. She had no idea who was coming towards her. She remained where she was, surprisingly relaxed considering she didn't know what was coming. Then it struck her. She wasn't relaxed. She was lethargic and risked succumbing to the drugged wine. It looked like Elvera had gone through with her threat. The dose was a lot stronger now.

The footsteps stopped in front of Esther. "Remove that necklace she is wearing," Elvera demanded.

"I don't think-"

Elvera interrupted the woman. "Then don't. I pay you to take care of problems, not think."

"You pay me to be your PA," the woman said dryly.

"Same difference," Elvera said. "Now, remove the necklace."

Esther felt fingers at her neck and was almost grateful for the drugged wine that kept her motionless. Otherwise, she would have been tempted to draw back from the cold fingers.

"This would have to be the strangest request yet," the PA said.

"Get on with the task. I don't need your opinion on it. You're wasting time and I need you to take those signed documents back to the head office."

The PA spoke under her breath. She was close enough to Esther for her to hear the muttered words. "You never do want my opinion."

Esther felt the necklace being removed and wanted to grab it. The moment her throat was bare, she heard retreating footsteps. Who was leaving and who had been left behind? The mattress dipped as someone settled in beside her. Wild plans raced through her mind. None of them would help. Her body felt like lead. There was no way she could move. A warm breath brushed her lips and for a moment everything went blank. The next thing she knew she was rising from the bed, no longer in control of her body.

She wanted to scream. Better yet, she wanted to sink the executioner daggers into Elvera's body that was lying on the bed she'd vacated. But she could do none of that.

She chuckled, turning to Norman who stood in the doorway. "The girl fights. I'm surprised she can manage at all with how strong a dose we added to the wine."

"Do you need more wine?" Norman asked.

"No. She isn't strong enough to break free. Let her see how little she can do against me. There's nothing I've planned to do today that will cause problems if she observes it."

Esther spent the day visiting some of the many businesses Elvera's company owned. At each place, Norman introduced her as Elvera's heir. She wanted to deny his words. Wanted to beg someone to help her. She was powerless.

All she could do was observe. Then she realised Elvera was mistaken. She learned a lot of important information. Passwords, locations of the businesses, names of staff members and details about how each business was run. She had no idea how the information would help, but she kept listening so she could learn every little thing possible. In case there were weaknesses she'd be able to exploit.

It was well into the night when they returned home and Esther took an empty wine glass from Norman, pricking her finger and letting several drops fall into the glass, wishing she could protest. She placed it on the coffee table before striding to the bedroom and lying on the bed facing Elvera's body.

Even after Elvera left her, not only leaving her body, but also striding from the room, Esther continued to lie on the bed. She drew in a shaky breath, trying to hold herself together. For once screams and the crackle of flames didn't echo in her mind. No, Elvera's words, the way she spoke to people and the tone of her voice, filled it instead. There'd been times during the day when her voice hadn't sounded like her own. That had terrified her. How long would it be until she was no longer herself? She closed her eyes tightly. There had to be something she could do.

Pain shot through her and she squeezed her eyes closed as she fought against it, refusing to give Elvera the satisfaction of calling out and letting her know how much the consumption of her blood had affected her. The pain ebbed, replaced by anger. Opening her eyes, she forced herself out of the bed. She refused to lie here waiting for Elvera to finish the job of claiming her body. She tried both the door and window. They were still locked. A glance around the room showed there was nothing in here that could help. Something she'd learned earlier. Nothing had changed.

Exhaustion tugged at her. She strode to the bathroom, turning on the tap of the vanity and splashing water on her face, refusing to give in and collapse on the bed like her body demanded. About to leave the bathroom, her attention was caught by a small window above the toilet.

She stood on the toilet seat to take a closer look. She had no idea if she could manage, but she wasn't going to let that stop her. She slid the louvres out of the window and leaned them against the wall, taking a deep breath before she tried to squeeze through the extremely small opening. She angled her shoulders through. Hope rose. It was tight, but it looked like she could do this. Hope plummeted when her hips became stuck. She tried to lever herself out, pushing against the outside wall, dreading to think what would happen if she managed to slip through the opening and land on the ground below.

She couldn't budge. She was stuck half in and half out the window. Frustration and anger filled her and again she wanted to scream. Her hands clenched into fists as she pushed against the outside of the house. She was so close to freedom. Unshed tears burned her eyes. She blinked rapidly as an ache formed in her throat. She'd expected it to be fire. Expected to eventually be taken by the thing she'd once escaped. She supposed there was no way she could have known that demons existed. She took inventory. She had nothing with her. No weapon and no phone. Not even the cross Malachi had given her. Not that it had helped this time. She raised a hand to look at one of the marks at the pulse point of her wrist, barely visible in the limited light that reached her from the neighbouring house.

She had killed a demon. Or severed it from this existence. Which as far as she was concerned was the same as killing one. Surely she could escape from one little window considering all she'd done. She tried again, pushing and pulling and struggling to break free. The window frame scraped against bones and flesh. She ignored the pain. Worse would come if she remained. Far worse.

She breathed in sharply as she broke free, sliding headfirst towards the ground. She put out her hands to break her fall. Arms wrapped around her, a body cushioning her. Panic faded as she realised it was Malachi and she returned his embrace.

His arms tightened around her. "I had to wait until they left. They would have noticed if I'd come too close while they were here."

"They're gone?" She drew back from him, remaining on the ground. "The three of them?"

Malachi nodded. "I don't know for how long." He scrambled to his feet, holding out a hand to her. "Blake is a couple of streets over, waiting for us."

"Where did they go? What time is it?"

"Nearly midnight." He continued to hold out a hand to her. "We have to go."

"Why would they go out so late?"

Malachi reached forward to grasp her hand. "We can worry about that later. All I know is another demon turned up and they left. Including the fourth demon."

She let him draw her to her feet, trying to figure out what Elvera might be planning. Nothing she'd done all day indicated she'd go out tonight. "What if it's important? What if it's something we need to know about? We should search the house while they're gone."

Malachi stared at her for a moment, eventually

chuckling. "And people say I like to live dangerously."

"It's not living dangerously. It's the opposite."

Malachi tugged her towards the street. "It doesn't make sense to search the house." He took out his phone and sent a short text.

"Who did you message? And of course it makes sense. Something must have happened. We need to know what."

"Blake will pick us up out the front in less than a minute." He continued towards the footpath.

She drew out of his grip, stopping where she was to glare at him. "I'm not going anywhere until I find out what's going on."

"There's no guarantee you'll learn anything new by searching Elvera's house."

"I have to do something." She tried to ignore the fear she could hear in her voice, but it was impossible. She wanted to beg him to tell her everything would be okay. She doubted she'd believe him even if he did.

Malachi came close, lowering his voice. "You're not alone."

She started to protest, but wasn't sure exactly what she'd be protesting. She didn't need his help? She'd always been alone? She'd never been good at working as part of a team. She'd had so little opportunity to do so.

Blake pulled up, stepping out of his vehicle and striding towards them. "Ready to go?"

Esther shook her head.

Malachi spoke before she had the chance. "She's worried about what they're planning. Another demon turned up."

Blake turned to Esther. "If it helps, he's the one we were following earlier. I had a look on the map while I was waiting for you. I also had a look when we arrived. There was only one blood spot in the house. It left first. Coming past where we were parked. It was Nethod."

"How are we meant to find her?" Esther demanded. "I refuse to spend the rest of my life running."

"You won't," Malachi promised.

"How can you say that?" She met Malachi's gaze, trying to see if he was only telling her that to get her moving. "How can you believe that?" It was clear from the look in his eyes that he truly believed his words.

Malachi grinned. "If it's one thing I know, it's how to do my job." He took hold of her hand. "Which is why we have to get out of here. It makes no sense to stay and search the place."

Blake ran a hand along his left arm. "Doesn't matter if you did want to stay. There are demons headed this way. It feels like there are some powerful ones amongst them."

"How can you tell?" Esther glanced at Malachi. "And why didn't you say something?"

"He can't sense them from as far away as I can." Blake rolled back his sleeve to his elbow, revealing a demon mark that travelled further than the area he exposed, red barbs tattooed on it to make it look like barbed wire. "If you continue to hunt demons, you'll be able to notice them from a greater distance too."

Esther stared at Blake, even after he entered the vehicle. She didn't protest when Malachi helped her into the vehicle, dazed by what she'd seen. What had Blake gone through to have ended up with such a lengthy demon mark? And why had he tattooed it with red barbs? There was so much she didn't know. She thought of the book she'd stolen from Elvera. "Where is my handbag?"

"In the back." Malachi reached over the back of the seat and got it for her, dropping it in her lap. "Everything is still in it. But I do think you should let the daggers be put somewhere safe."

Blake glanced over his shoulder. "Unless you want to spend your life executing demons."

"No." Her answer was automatic. She frowned. What would it be like? Her gaze was drawn to the folded map, lying beside her on the seat, highlighted each time the vehicle was flooded with light when they passed a streetlight. Not that it mattered. She needed a job. The money from Norman and Elvera wouldn't last forever and she doubted they'd keep paying her each week.

Malachi took her hand, cradling it in his. "What's wrong?"

She shook her head rather than answer, drawing her hand from his light grip. She took one of the daggers out, her hand wrapping around the handle. It felt comfortable, like it was a part of her. "I need a better way of carrying these with me than in my handbag."

Malachi took the dagger from her, nearly dropping the weapon before handing it back. "What did you do to it?"

"What do you mean?"

"It's hot. Like it's been left on the dash of a car in summer during the middle of the day." Malachi examined his hand. "I half expected it to have caused blisters."

Esther ran a finger down the middle of the blade.

"It doesn't feel any different." She examined Malachi in the limited light. "Are you okay?"

Malachi laughed softly. "I've got a feeling I should be the one asking that question." He linked his fingers through hers, momentarily tightening his grip before letting go. "It's okay. We'll sort this out."

Chapter Twenty-One

Esther wanted to protest, but doubted Malachi would believe her. She was fine. There was nothing wrong with her that wouldn't be fixed by dealing with Elvera. Once that demon had her ties severed to all existence, everything would be fine. Yawning, she put the dagger away. She was too exhausted from the wine Elvera had given her.

Malachi slipped an arm around her shoulders and drew her close. "Sleep. We'll figure out what to do after we've slept."

She started to argue, changing her mind and sinking against him instead. "A bed would be good." She closed her eyes. Although she had to admit, snuggling up to Malachi was nice.

Esther had no memory of falling asleep, but when the vehicle coming to a stop woke her, she guessed that at some stage she must have. Blinking she straightened, pulling away from the warmth of Malachi's body. "What are we doing?"

Blake looked over his shoulder. "Breakfast and change of driver." He grinned. "I was debating whether or not I should wake you or just let Scarlett and Jesse borrow my vehicle."

Malachi reached for the door handle. "We're both awake now. We can swap vehicles."

It didn't take long for them to say goodbye to Blake and join Jesse and Scarlett in their vehicle that was parked ahead of them. Scarlett was in the driver's seat while Jesse sat beside her in the passenger seat.

Jesse turned to face them the moment they were seated. "There's food in the esky on the floor." He paused a moment. "How was your night?"

"Should the daggers be hot to touch?" Malachi asked.

Jesse turned further in the seat. "Show me."

"There's nothing wrong with them," Esther protested.

Jesse's lips curved into a half smile. "Then it won't matter if you show them to me."

Esther glared at Malachi when he chuckled softly. "I'm not giving them up. I need them." How else was she meant to beat Elvera?

Jesse held out a hand. "They're yours to do with as you wish. I have no plans to take them from you."

Esther examined him carefully before nodding and handing over one of the daggers. Although his expression barely changed, she caught something in it that had her worried. "What's wrong with it?"

Jesse returned the dagger, rubbing his palm against the leg of his jeans. "They've begun the bonding process."

Esther held onto the dagger rather than put it away. "What does that mean exactly?"

"The more you use them," Jesse nodded to the dagger she held, "or even handle them, the quicker the bond will form."

Esther looked from the dagger to Jesse and back again. "Which means?"

"That with how quickly the bond is forming, you have days at the most to make a decision as to what you want to do." Jesse waited until she met his gaze before he continued to speak. "Do you want to be a demon executioner or do you want to return to your previous life once Elvera no longer hunts you?"

She ran a finger down the centre of the blade. It felt like it vibrated beneath her fingertips. She almost asked what the dagger was made from, but decided it wasn't important. After returning the dagger to the box, she looked at Jesse again. "How do demon executioners afford to live? I doubt anyone pays them to go after demons." She frowned. "Or do they?"

Jesse shrugged. "I don't know how they do it now. There were always spoils of war in previous centuries."

Esther found herself frowning again. "What war?"

Malachi captured her hand, sliding his fingers through hers to momentarily squeeze her hand before letting go. "Jesse is referring to the war against demons. There are other demons like Elvera who have money and holdings in this world."

It took Esther a moment to answer. She'd needed to process the information. "I could make a living hunting demons?"

"Would you want to?"

Malachi's words had been so soft she'd needed to lean closer to hear them. "I don't know. It'd make a change from being fired for fighting."

Malachi chuckled, the sound echoed by Jesse. Once more Malachi reached for her hand, lightly squeezing before letting go. "It's dangerous."

"That's nothing new," she muttered. Life tended to be full of danger and no guarantees. How many times had she been worried a fight would end up putting her in hospital? Yet she'd fought anyway, refusing to back down.

Malachi held her gaze. "Are you seriously considering this? If you want to hunt demons, I can ask Luca to teach you. You don't have to become an executioner. We don't know what that'll mean for you. What it would mean for any human."

"Power. That thing that every demon craves and tries to amass." Jesse glanced at Scarlett. "Or at least most demons."

"Power?" Esther studied Jesse, trying to figure out what he meant. "As in I would become a demon?" She didn't like the thought of that.

Jesse shook his head. "No, as in you would gain some of the strength of those you execute. Gain a small fraction of their abilities. Able to move faster, physically stronger, heal quicker, see better and eventually hear the proverbial pin drop."

"That doesn't sound too bad." The smell of smoke filled her memories along with the crackle of flames, reminders of all she'd lost. She hadn't been strong enough. If her strength had been greater, would they still be here?

Scarlett, who'd remained silent throughout the discussion, her attention focused on the busy road ahead, glanced over her shoulder. "There's always a downside. Why don't you share the negative effects with Esther?"

"I don't know that they'd be perceived as a negative side effect," Jesse said. "The power a demon can gain from killing an executioner is phenomenal. Which makes them a target. As an executioner, that can only be a good thing. It'd save you having to track them down. They'd come to you."

"You have a strange way of looking at things, Jes," Scarlett said.

Esther was tempted to point out that although Jesse might have a strange way of looking at things, Scarlett seemed like she tended to understate things. She looked away when Jesse laughed softly, running a finger down Scarlett's cheek.

"You need to make a decision quickly," Malachi said. "Leave it too long and it could be made for you."

Esther thought of all the decisions in her life that had been made for her. Ones she'd been given no say in. She was sick of that happening. But how could she make a decision when she had no idea about exactly what being a demon executioner meant.

"Esther?"

She met Malachi's gaze, instantly looking away from the concern she saw in his eyes. "I will. I just need more information first."

"Have you read the book you took from Elvera?" Jesse asked.

Esther stared at her handbag. She'd partially forgotten about the book. "No." She took it out, trying not to think about the cover. It didn't help when the first page she read detailed the sacrifice of the woman whose skin had been used on the book and the ritual that had been used to extend the life of the book.

Esther read over every single word, some of them difficult to decipher. It took the entire day. She continued to read when Scarlett and Jesse changed places so Jesse could drive and remained in the back when they were replaced by Luca and Penelope. They were the two hunters who'd been with Malachi when she'd first encountered Nethod and Torrnon.

About halfway through the book, Esther found a page she kept returning to, rereading parts of it. When she eventually reached the end of the book, she closed it, resting it on her lap.

"What plan did you come up with?" Malachi asked.

"Nothing." Esther's gaze was drawn to the book. "At least I don't think I have."

"It's dangerous, isn't it," Malachi stated.

Luca chuckled. "I would have thought that would be your type of plan."

"There's a potion. One that negates the effects of the one Elvera puts in the wine. It's also used when she takes over my body for the last time and evicts me from it. If I drink it first, it won't stop her from being able to possess me, but I'd be aware of everything right down to the moment she left my body and is vulnerable as she settles back into hers." Esther breathed in slowly and steadily, trying to ignore the sickening feeling that washed over her. "I can attack then. And she won't be ready for it. All I'd need is for someone to put the daggers in the room, two of them under the pillow so I can use them on her."

"I doubt they'll leave her alone," Malachi said.

"Norman goes everywhere with her. Including when she's in my body." Esther shuddered. She really hated thinking about it.

Penelope looked over her shoulder. "Where would you find the potion? Or would you have to make it?"

"I think I know exactly where to find it." Esther smiled wryly. "Which means someone needs to lure Elvera and Norman away so I can get into her safe again."

"She might have changed the password," Malachi said.

Esther looked him over. "You don't want me to do this."

Malachi smiled. "Not really. I think there are too many things that might go wrong."

"Do you think I should let her take my body?" Esther demanded. "Kick me from it so she can have it for herself."

"No." Malachi captured her hand, cradling it in his. "Never."

"Then what?" Esther demanded.

"You need to find a way to make her drink your blood to make certain the daggers will work on her," Malachi said. "In case the extrication process isn't enough."

"She already has." Again Esther shuddered as she recalled her blood dripping into the wine glass.

Penelope turned in her seat, facing them. "What do you need help with?"

Luca momentarily reached out to brush his hand along Penelope's arm before speaking. "We can lure them away if you would trust us with that task."

Esther looked at each of the hunters in the vehicle, her gaze resting on Malachi last. "Well?"

He tightened his grip on her hand. "I will do everything in my power to make sure you're victorious."

"Why can't she be sent to hell like every other demon?" Penelope asked. "Wouldn't that be easier?"

"It's an extrication rather than a straight forward possession. She's as bound to this world as any other human," Malachi said. "Hell is no longer considered her home. Nothing we do will send her there."

Esther drew in a deep breath, straightening her shoulders. "Daggers it is then." She released her breath slowly. "When can we start?" She wasn't about to spend the rest of her life hunted by Elvera. She already had enough things keeping her awake of a night without adding that to the list.

Malachi's phone rang, interrupting him. "What's wrong?" He paused a moment. "That's a pretty big incentive." He was silent for almost a minute. "Thanks for letting me know." He returned his phone to a pocket of his jeans, his gaze meeting Esther's.

"What did they want?" She supposed she probably should have started by asking who it had been.

"You aren't safe," Malachi said.

All she could do was look at him for a moment. "Haven't you been paying attention? I haven't been safe since I took the job with Elvera."

"Things are worse." Malachi lowered his voice before he spoke. "We will protect you."

She recognised that tone. It was the one people used before telling you really bad news. Like the death of someone close. "What happened?"

Malachi cradled her hand in his before he spoke. "Elvera has offered to provide a blood sacrifice to whichever demon brings you to her. Unharmed." He barely paused before continuing. "And a blood sacrifice for each of the daggers returned as well as the grimoire."

"What is a blood sacrifice?" Esther asked.

"A human sacrificed to a particular demon. It provides them with a lot of power." Malachi's hands tightened around hers. "We won't let them get you."

Luca pulled over onto the side of the road, turning to face them. "Once Elvera no longer exists, this offer will not be valid."

"Why are we pulling over?" Esther scanned the area, but could see no reason why they should have stopped.

Penelope swung open the door. "My turn to drive."

Esther watched as the two of them exited the vehicle and walked around to the front, pausing to wrap their arms around each other. "Is it safe to stop here for so long?"

Malachi laughed softly. "They won't be long. Luca is a brilliant battle tactician." He paused a moment. "Esther?"

She faced him, more than enough light from the nearby streetlight to see his expression. She had no idea what it meant, at least he no longer looked or sounded like he was about to share more bad news with her.

"Once this is over, would you like to go out somewhere with me?"

Chapter Twenty-Two

Esther stared at Malachi. It hadn't been anything like what she'd expected him to say. "Like a date?"

He grinned. "Yeah, like a date."

Before Esther could reply, Luca and Penelope climbed in the four-wheel-drive, Penelope starting the engine.

Once Luca had his seatbelt on, he faced them. "We don't need to draw them away, just make sure they're unable to notice you in the vicinity." He nodded his head towards Esther. "If enough demon hunters came knocking on Elvera's door, it'd make it difficult for her to tell who was or wasn't nearby."

Esther opened her mouth several times before she was able to speak. "You want me to break into Elvera's house while she's at home."

Luca inclined his head. "It would be unexpected. We could turn up there demanding your return. Tell her that demons snatched you from us and we want you back. Her powers would be less than usual during the extrication process. If no others have your blood, this would be our best option."

The longer Luca spoke, the more his words began to make sense to Esther. "This might work."

Penelope laughed. "Of course it will work. Luca has had centuries of practice at this kind of thing."

The words startled Esther. "You're a demon too?"

Luca shook his head. "I was born human."

"Should we organise it?" Malachi asked.

Esther looked at each of them. She wanted to say yes. Wanted to do anything that would get her out of this mess. But that was how she'd ended up in this mess in the first place. Agreeing to something that looked good on the surface. "What are the negatives?"

"You might be caught and Elvera only has to possess you two more times before your body is hers."

She closed her eyes at Malachi's words, trying not to give into the panic they caused.

"Esther?"

His soft tone calmed her and she opened her eyes. "Let's do this. I want my life back."

"Keep using those daggers and it might not be the

same life you had before meeting Elvera," Malachi said.

His words replayed in her mind, causing her lips to slowly curve into a smile. "You know, that might not be such a bad thing."

Malachi took out his phone again. "Are you completely certain you want to do this?"

Images from her life flicked through her mind. She had the fleeting thought that you were meant to see scenes from your life as it ended. She pushed it aside. "Yes. Elvera isn't getting my body and she's certainly not getting the chance to make five blood sacrifices to demons. Those daggers are mine." She felt a warmth at the pulse point of her wrists and looked down. A passing streetlight highlighted the marks. Had they grown? She dismissed the thought. It didn't matter. Elvera was about to be wiped from existence and those daggers were her only means of doing it. She looked up, meeting Malachi's gaze. "Let's get this party started."

Malachi grinned. "I'll make some calls."

It took longer than Esther expected for everything to be organised. Long enough for her to change her mind several times and worry about what might happen. No wonder she preferred action over thinking and planning. It left too much time for doubts to surface.

Malachi's phone rang and Esther sighed. It had been ringing and signalling incoming messages for hours. She checked her own phone. It was two in the morning. It'd be daylight before they could do anything. She sighed again, looking at Malachi when he put his phone away, wishing she'd been paying attention to his end of the call when she saw his expression. There was mischief in his eyes and he grinned at her. "It's time?"

Malachi nodded. "It's time."

Penelope dropped them at the corner, continuing towards Elvera's house once they were out of the vehicle. Esther stood on the footpath, feeling like she might throw up and wishing she hadn't left her handbag behind. Before she could tell Malachi she couldn't do it, he slid his fingers through hers, lightly squeezing her hand.

"You ready?"

She examined his expression, barely visible in the limited light. "You're looking forward to this."

"I'd rather you didn't go in there, but other than that, yeah, I am."

"I'd prefer you didn't go in there either." Esther

walked beside Malachi. "I don't want you getting caught."

"Then I guess we make sure we're not discovered raiding the safe."

As they approached Elvera's home, Esther caught sight of the demanding crowd at the front door. Remaining in the shadows, she kept glancing at the many demon hunters gathered together. "How many are here?" She kept her voice low even though it would be unlikely anyone could hear her over the noise of the crowd.

"About fifty." Malachi led the way down the side of the house. "Give or take a few."

"All of them live in Brisbane?"

Malachi laughed softly. "Some of them live in Brisbane. Some came from neighbouring areas. But we do have enough who live here to overflow a church if we all turned up to mass at the same time."

She struggled to imagine a family so large. Even when her parents had been alive, her family hadn't been large. She doubted there were many families as large as Malachi's. Reaching the back of the house, she crept along the verandah, pausing before she reached the back door. She peered inside. No one. But she could clearly hear everyone at the front door.

"You sure you want to go through with this?"

Malachi asked. "I know where the safe is. I can get the potion for you."

She didn't bother answering. He'd soon learn she wasn't the sort to let someone else take care of things for her. Slipping inside, a smile half formed. They had a date when this was over. She had no idea what to expect, but assumed it would be interesting. What did demon hunters do on their days off? Reaching the entrance to the wide hallway that led to the front door, she peered around it. Norman and Elvera faced the crowd, arguing with them. The distance she needed to cover before reaching the stairs leading to the next floor, seemed to be growing lengthier by the second.

Malachi lightly touched Esther on the shoulder, indicating he would go first.

She hesitated, then nodded. Her gaze followed his figure as he lightly crossed the hallway, keeping close to the wall. As he headed up the stairs, she let out the breath she'd been holding, scurrying after him. She was halfway there when Elvera started to turn towards her. She froze.

"I've wasted more than enough time on all of you. I have no idea where Esther is, but even if I did, I would not turn her over to any of you."

Allie grabbed hold of Elvera's arm. "We're not finished talking."

Norman took a step forward, halted by Elvera raising a hand and waving him back.

Blake placed his hand on Allie's shoulder. "Let her go, Allie cat."

Allie glared at Elvera. "Tell me where Esther is." She let go of Elvera.

Esther scurried along the rest of the hallway, collapsing against the wall of the stairwell once she was out of sight. She pressed a hand against her chest. It didn't slow the rapid beat of her heart.

Malachi tugged her upwards, his hand clasping hers, his eyes filled with worry.

She looked away from his gaze, feeling like she should apologise. She couldn't believe she'd frozen like that. At least it would have only been her caught since Malachi had gone ahead. Her legs were unsteady as she continued up the stairs, the crackle of fire filling her mind. She fought the urge to turn around and head to the ground floor. She hated multi-storey buildings. They were dangerous.

Malachi spoke as they approached the locked door, keeping his voice low. "Are you sure you're okay? I can do this if you want to leave. I'm not the one she wants."

"I will be okay. Once Elvera is dead." And she was out of this house. It felt like the walls were closing in on her and it was definitely warmer up here. She typed in the password, swinging the door open and hurrying across the room to the safe, relieved the password hadn't been changed.

Malachi waited in the doorway, looking between Esther and the hallway.

She kept glancing over her shoulder to check he was okay. She typed in the pin number. Nothing happened. She stared at the number pad. Had Elvera changed it or had she mistyped the numbers. Fighting the urge to check on Malachi again, she focused on the number pad, pressing each number carefully. She clung to the edge of the safe when the pin number worked.

Malachi ran lightly towards her, holding up his phone. "Elvera closed the door. They couldn't keep her distracted any longer. We have to go."

Esther shook her head. "I need the potion." She opened the safe, checking through the bottles.

"Hurry." Malachi returned to the doorway.

It was the fifth bottle she checked, the label written in the same handwriting that had been used in the book. The bottle wasn't overly large, it would fit in her pocket. Checking several of the other smaller bottles, she noticed there were a few doses of it. She took a second one since they had to be taken anywhere up to four hours before being possessed for it to work. Closing the safe, she took a step towards Malachi.

"What are you doing here?" Elvera demanded.

Esther froze.

"I was looking for Esther. You didn't think we were going to let you keep her, did you?" Malachi stepped away from the doorway and out of sight.

Esther ran her fingers across the bottles she'd shoved in her pocket. She couldn't let anything happen to Malachi. As long as Elvera tried to possess her within the next four hours, everything would work out. She downed the contents of one of the bottles, Malachi and Elvera arguing over him being in her house, Norman joining the conversation. She dropped the potion bottles in the back of one of the filing cabinet drawers, not wanting to risk Elvera finding them on her, before stepping into the hallway.

Elvera stopped halfway through her sentence. "What are you doing here?" She looked at Malachi. "I thought you said you were looking for her."

Esther joined Malachi, standing shoulder to shoulder with him. "He was. I came after him. But

I'm not about to let him face you while I hide in the study. If you let him go, I'll stay here willingly. At least until the sun rises."

Elvera inclined her head. "Norman, escort him outside."

Malachi tried to break free from Norman's grip when he grabbed hold of him. "Esther. Not–"

"Go. She still has to possess me another two times. Do you think I'm about to stick around long enough for that to happen?" Esther asked.

Malachi met her gaze, looking over his shoulder as Norman marched him down the hallway. "You better not. We have a date when all this is over."

Elvera laughed. "How sweet." Her lips twisted into a smile. "That will not be happening. I would never go on a date with someone like you." She looked Malachi up and down. "A demon hunter."

Norman dragged Malachi out of view and Esther nearly bolted after him. Her hands clenched into fists as she forced herself to remain where she stood. "I won't let you win. This is my body and I'm nowhere near finished with it."

Again Elvera laughed, heading for the stairs. "We shall see." She glanced over her shoulder. "Don't keep me waiting. I'll have Norman pour a glass of wine for you since you seem so eager to stay with me."

She hurried after Elvera. Not because she was eager to get it over and done with, but because she wanted to be on the ground floor. Her steps slowed as she reached the downstairs hallway, her gaze drawn to the front door. She desperately wanted to leave. Wanted to run as far from Elvera as possible. Her shoulders straightened and she continued to her room. If she ran now, she'd spend the rest of her life running. That wasn't going to happen.

Sensing someone behind her, Esther spun to see Norman standing in the doorway, holding a full glass of wine. He remained silent, his expression neutral. It took her a moment to walk towards him and take the glass from his hand. She held his gaze as she drank the contents, keeping her own expression blank. Finished, she held out the glass. There was a drop of red in the bottom. It reminded her of blood.

Norman took the glass, striding from the room without a word.

Chapter Twenty-Three

Esther stared at the empty doorway. Weren't they going to lock her in? She took a step towards the exit, staggering when exhaustion washed over her. Stumbling to the bed, she blinked as she tried to bring the room into focus. How much had they given her? Panic washed through her as she dropped onto the bed. Had she taken enough of the other potion for her plan to work? Darkness crashed over her.

She had no idea how long had passed, or what Elvera had been doing, but she became aware of her surroundings while sitting in an intimate restaurant, Norman across from her. She raised a glass of wine to her lips, looking at Norman over the brim. "Not long now and this pesky child will have been dealt with. I feel we should take a journey somewhere we haven't been before. I'm sure there must be somewhere on this earth I haven't yet seen."

Esther drank the wine, letting Elvera do as she wished. This time, Elvera could be in charge. Soon enough it would be her turn. Then Elvera would never be a problem again.

Norman nodded. "I will see what I can find."

Esther placed the wine glass on the table. "Good." She rose to her feet. "Take me home. I have been in control long enough for today. Once more and she will be mine. There will be no waiting after the second possession. You will have the other potion ready and I will immediately take control of her body."

"I'll watch her personally between possessions. She won't escape this time." Norman walked behind Esther, stepping ahead as they reached the door and opening it for her.

The drive to the house was silent and she watched the passing scenery out the window, the early morning light creating just as many shadows as it banished. She reminded herself to remain calm. She'd only have one chance at this. One chance to escape Elvera's plans. The next time she possessed her would be the last. She couldn't let it get to that.

Reaching the house, she headed to her bedroom, the place silent and empty. Kicking off her high heels, she lay on the bed, facing Elvera. The woman's eyes were closed and she was on her side, her chest barely rising and falling. Closing her eyes, she felt her lips twist into a smile.

"You're mine, Esther. One more time and you're mine." It felt weird to speak the words seemingly to herself. Her first instinct was to argue, instead she relaxed, breathing out slowly.

She felt Elvera leave her. Like her skin fit more snugly and the world no longer felt distant. Opening her eyes, she slipped her hand under her pillow, hearing soft footsteps behind her. Fear rushed through her when she couldn't find anything under the pillow. Where were the daggers?

The thought of them made a sensation vibrate through her, like a compass turning and letting her know they were nearby. Her gaze was caught by the pillow Elvera's head rested upon. Slipping her hand under it, she felt the handle of a dagger, grabbing hold of it as Elvera's eyes opened.

Elvera blinked several times, looking disorientated.

Esther drew her hand out from under the pillow, bringing the dagger with her. Rising up, she drove the dagger towards Elvera's heart. A hand clamped around her wrist well before she could make contact.

"Let it go." Norman's voice was soft, but easily

heard since he moved in close, his other arm sliding around her waist to imprison her.

Elvera struggled to rise, her body unusually uncoordinated.

Esther looked from the dagger to Elvera. She'd failed. Anger rushed through her and she wanted to strike out at something. Preferably Elvera. Her other hand curled into a fist.

"Drop it," Norman ordered.

She started to argue, her lips curving into a smile instead. Letting go of the dagger, she snatched it out of the air with her other hand, driving the blade into Elvera's chest. Her smile vanished at the flow of blood, shock racing through her that she'd somehow managed to grab the dagger from mid-air without cutting herself like she'd expected. But she'd been willing to risk it.

Norman's arm tightened around her, his roar echoing around the room.

Elvera tried to grasp the dagger, but drew her hands back from the weapon with a soft sound.

Esther struggled to escape Norman's grip, her vision darkening around the edges as his arm tightened around her and it became difficult to breathe. She pulled the dagger from Elvera, not letting go of it even as she fought to escape Norman.

Pain and heat shot across her wrists, like someone had run a hot blade over them. She reached for the second dagger that had been hidden beneath Elvera's pillow, barely managing to scratch the woman with it. She didn't know if that would be enough. She tried to sink it into her as she'd done with the first one.

Norman flung Esther aside before the second dagger could make contact again, lifting Elvera to cradle her body. The words he murmured against her hair were impossible to hear.

Esther staggered to her feet, her grip tightening on both daggers. She gulped in air, swaying as she watched Norman. She had no idea what she'd do if he attacked. She took a step back. About to run, she was frozen in place by pain washing over her, immobilising her. The sharp pain went as quickly as it arrived.

Norman lowered Elvera to the bed and faced Esther.

She backed away at the expression on his face. Anger and shock. She wasn't about to wait around for him to get past the shock of losing Elvera and attack her. Spinning, she ran for the back door, transferring the dagger from her right hand to her left, barely managing to hold the two of them in the one hand. Reaching the door, she flung it open.

"Esther," Norman called out from behind her.

She hesitated, looking from the backyard to Norman who seemed too calm as he walked towards her.

"Esther."

She faced the backyard at hearing Malachi call her name.

"We have to go. Several demons are headed this way." Malachi strode towards her. "Blake is out the front waiting for us."

"Wait, Esther," Norman called out.

She wasn't that crazy. Shaking her head, she ran towards Malachi, grabbing his hand as she reached him, continuing towards the side yard. They were nearly at the vehicle when she remembered the third dagger. "I have to go back." She tried to pull away from him.

He tightened his grip. "You removed a demon from existence that Norman has spent centuries with."

"Esther!"

She glanced over her shoulder when Norman called out to her. "I need the other dagger."

"We'll come back for it another time." Reaching the vehicle, Malachi opened the back door. "With other hunters."

Blake, who had the engine running, wound down the window. "He's following."

Malachi ushered her into the vehicle. "We'll come back."

"When?" She stared out the back window at Norman who stood on the edge of the footpath, his clothes and body streaked with blood. She continued to watch him until they turned a corner and she lost sight of him.

"This afternoon," Malachi said. "Before stronger demons can roam the world."

Blake glanced over his shoulder. "What are you planning?"

Malachi explained. "Are you in?"

"I have other plans. Scarlett and Jesse could help. They have nothing on today," Blake said.

Before Esther could agree with his suggestion, Malachi lifted her right hand, turning it to look at her wrist. She stared at the mark that had formed, slashing across her wrist. Turning her other hand, she saw there was a mark the same length on that wrist too, blood smeared across it and her hand. "Is that a problem?"

Malachi shrugged. "Maybe Jesse will know." Letting go of her hand, he took out his phone and sent a message.

She continued to stare at her hands, the blood drying on her skin. "I need to clean up."

"I'll take you to Gran's," Blake said.

Malachi sent another message. "I'll let Scarlett and Jesse know. See if they can meet us there."

When they arrived at Gran's house, Jesse met them out the front, lifting Esther's blood-streaked hand. She'd made an attempt at cleaning it, but there was still too much blood on her skin. As well as having splattered her clothes. She wanted to pull away from his grip, not sure she wanted to know what the longer mark meant. Especially with how intently he stared at her wrist.

Jesse nodded to the daggers she clutched in her right hand. "Use them again and you will become an executioner." He let go of her hand. "You would spend the rest of your life hunting down demons who other demons find too evil to remain in existence."

"How can you be certain?" What would she do about Nethod if she couldn't use the daggers? He would keep coming after her. She had no doubt of that.

"The mark is half complete." Jesse gestured towards her wrist.

"Half complete?" She examined her wrist before returning her attention to Jesse.

"They aren't demon marks. They make a single band around your wrist. One on each wrist, shackling you to the daggers for the rest of your life. Slave to their need to remove the worst of demons from existence," Jesse said.

Her grip tightened on the daggers she held. "We left one of them behind."

"It will call to you." Jesse met her gaze. "Can you sense where each one is?"

"How do you do that?"

"Think of them. Think of each individual dagger." Jesse moved closer, lowering his voice before he spoke again. "Can you sense where they are?"

She barely had to try. It was like a vibration in her mind. "Yes."

"Then you are closer to becoming an executioner than I thought." Jesse gestured towards the daggers again. "You might be best giving them into someone else's keeping if you don't want to complete the process."

She automatically moved her hand further from him, barely managing not to hide the daggers behind her back or blurt out the word 'no'. It was close. "How can I protect myself without them?"

"You'd be safer without them. Demons will be

drawn to them. Ones that fear you and will hunt you before you can hunt them," Jesse said.

Malachi slipped an arm around her shoulders. "We won't leave you unprotected."

She stepped away from him, meeting his gaze. She didn't have it in her to sit around and wait for others to protect her. "I need the other dagger."

"There will be no going back," Jesse warned.

"I can arrange for someone to teach you how to fight demons without using the daggers," Malachi said. "There are plenty of hunters who could teach you. Not just Luca."

Blake joined them. "There are other ways."

She looked at each of them, surprised to see the concern in both Blake and Malachi's eyes. She wanted to protest that they didn't know her. The words died unspoken as she thought of how she'd feel if something happened to one of them. Especially to Malachi.

"Esther?" Malachi captured her hand, squeezing it lightly. "What do you want to do?"

She examined his expression. Other than the worry, she could see no other emotions. Well, maybe curiosity, but that was it. "You aren't going to tell me why I should choose your way?"

Malachi grinned. "Your life. You're the one who

has to live with the consequences. After all you've read, you should have a good idea about the negatives."

"What about the positives?" Esther asked.

Malachi's grin didn't falter. "Mine are probably different to yours."

"If you had the chance, would you choose to use the daggers?" Esther asked.

Malachi shook his head. "I have no need of them." He grinned. "But if they were my only method of going after demons…" He shrugged, letting his voice trail off.

"Why do you fight them?" Esther looked at Jesse and Blake too. "All of you. Why do any of you fight demons?"

"Our reasons won't be your reasons," Blake said.

The front door opened and Scarlett stepped outside. "Is something wrong?"

Jesse moved to Scarlett's side. "No more than usual, Lady Knight."

Scarlett looked from Jesse to Esther and back again. "Are we going after the dagger? Gran doesn't like the idea of it being left where a demon can find it. Even without the three of them being together a single dagger is too powerful to be left in the hands of a demon."

Chapter Twenty-Four

Straightening her shoulders, Esther met Scarlett's gaze. "We're going after the dagger." She looked at each of the hunters with her. She had no idea why they'd chosen to be hunters, but not a single one of them looked like they were dissatisfied with their choice. It would be nice to know what that felt like.

"Are you sure?" Malachi's words were low.

Esther faced him, thinking over his words. "Yeah. I am." A shiver ran through her. For a moment, she thought it was fear. It had been so long since she'd felt anticipation for anything, that she hadn't initially recognised it.

Scarlett took a step towards the front door. "I'll grab weapons."

They were organised within fifteen minutes and headed towards Elvera's house, Jesse and Scarlett in the front, Esther and Malachi in the back. She looked out the window. The blood had been cleaned from her body and she'd changed her clothes. Her hand rested on her handbag that was on the seat between her and Malachi. The book was inside, but the daggers were in sheaths Scarlett had found and that she'd strapped to her calves beneath her jeans. It wouldn't be quick to access them, but at least she wouldn't need to leave them behind. There was another sheath for when they managed to secure the third one.

The drive was silent and Esther was relieved. She had no idea what to talk about. All she could think of was the coming encounter. At least it drove all thoughts of crackling flames and the overpowering scent of smoke from her memories. Was she about to exchange one nightmare for another? She supposed she'd soon find out.

Reaching the house, Jesse pulled up out the front. They clambered out. Esther had considered leaving her handbag in the vehicle, not wanting the book anywhere near Norman, but she was more worried about leaving it unattended. She led the way to the front door, starting to reach for the keys in her handbag when she stopped in front of it.

The door swung open. Norman faced her, a document in one hand and the dagger on a wooden tray in the other. "I am surprised you left it this long to return for it."

Esther stared open-mouthed at him. What was going on? The words wouldn't form. She could only stand there gaping.

"When would you like me to make the appointment to see the lawyer?" Norman asked.

He had a slight scent of old smoke clinging to him, stronger than she'd ever noticed it before.

Malachi reached past Esther and took the document from Norman.

"Do you wish me to remove that from him or are you happy for him to read it?" Norman asked.

Esther shook her head, nodding instead when Norman started to reach for Malachi. "What is going on?" The words burst from her.

Malachi held the document out to Esther. "You're Elvera's heir."

"But…" Her voice trailed off and she slowly shook her head. "I killed her."

"I suggest you don't mention that to the police when they interview you," Norman said. "Everything is in place to make it look like she took her life rather than face the painful end her medical condition would cause."

Esther's gaze was drawn to the dagger. It looked

out of place on the tray that would normally be used to serve tea and scones. "I can take it?"

Norman inclined his head. "It is yours."

She snatched the dagger from the tray, half expecting someone to stop her.

"I have done what I can to call off the demons who were summoned to track you down. Not all were pleased by the outcome." Norman shrugged. "They should have moved quicker if they'd expected a different one. There is one who refuses to stop tracking you. Nethod. You severed his brother's ties to all existence."

"Why are you doing this?" Esther demanded.

"I am bound to the company you own." Norman gestured towards the document Malachi held. "You own me."

"You need to set him free," Scarlett said.

Norman glanced at Scarlett before returning his attention to Esther. "No."

"You want to remain bound to a company?" Scarlett asked. "To the owner of that company?"

Norman smiled, one that sent a shiver through Esther. "It suits me."

"You have to set him free," Scarlett said. "It won't matter what he's bound to. If he causes harm to humans, we will return him to hell. It'd be easier if he wasn't bound to something here."

Norman's smile vanished. "You will not interfere in matters that do not concern you, hunter."

Esther sheathed the dagger, feeling awkward being the only one holding a weapon. Not that it was any less awkward putting it away. "What am I meant to do with a demon?"

"Allow me to remain in this world and I'll serve you. Break the binding and I'll hunt you and remove you from this world," Norman promised.

The words he'd spoken to her when Elvera was in possession of her body returned. 'There's nothing for me in hell. Only pain.' She could see in his eyes that he meant every word he spoke. "I won't let you go after humans."

"You can't be thinking of letting him remain bound to your company," Scarlett said. "Actually, you can't be thinking of accepting the company."

"Things usually come with strings when given by a demon," Jesse warned.

"There are no strings." Norman again gestured towards the document. "That is Elvera's will. She was meant to be standing here, not Esther." He shrugged. "Plans change."

"You don't hate me for killing Elvera?" Esther

couldn't believe he could be so calm about it. Not after how he'd reacted earlier.

"I would prefer you dead, but the binding has me wanting to do your bidding." Norman paused for a moment. "I don't wish you dead for what you did to Elvera. Now I'm no longer bound to her through her company, my anger at her has returned. No, I wish you dead because you ruined other plans. That feeling will fade as the binding strengthens over the next few days."

Again Esther slowly shook her head. "This can't be happening."

Jesse gestured to where the daggers were sheathed and hidden. "You could set aside the daggers and leave it to Norman to deal with Nethod."

"No." The word escaped before she could consider the suggestion. Automatically escaped. She started to change what she'd said, remaining silent as she tried to figure out how she felt. Other than completely confused.

Norman smiled, a wistful one. "They get in your blood." The smile faded. "They were once meant to be mine. Until Elvera came into my life. Or Dazreyella as she was once known." He lifted Esther's hand, turning it so the mark on her wrist was clearly visible.

He'd moved too fast for her to avoid his action. She tried to pull out of his grip, meeting his gaze when his hand tightened on hers. "Let me go."

Norman did as she ordered, continuing to meet her gaze. "Setting them aside will not matter. They'll haunt your dreams for the rest of your days. They're in your blood, part of your soul. Accept them and that will be one less thing for you to be haunted by."

"What about being hunted by the demons she'll need to sever from existence if she does accept them?" Jesse asked.

Norman examined Jesse. "What haunts you with your whiff of demon about you?"

Jesse chuckled. "I'm not about to be distracted by your word games. I've played more than my share."

Malachi handed the document to Esther. "What do you want to do?"

She glanced over the document, seeing it was a copy of the will she'd already read. She returned it to Norman, trying to figure out what she should do. The daggers felt like they hummed against her body, through the sheaths. Calling for blood. Her hand curled into a fist at the rush of anger that washed over her at the thought of Nethod coming after her.

Norman smiled. A bone-chilling action.

Esther took a step back from him. "What are you thinking about?"

"It is more what you're thinking about. I can sense it. Your anger and anticipation at using the daggers on Nethod," Norman said.

"You can read my thoughts?" The moment the words were spoken, Esther felt like she should have protested his comment instead.

"Only a slight sense of your emotions. It will strengthen, but I'll never be able to read your mind or gain a full sense of your emotions," Norman said. "The binding hasn't been created to allow that. Only enough that I was able to know how best to serve Dazreyella."

"What do you plan to do?" Jesse glanced skywards. "It's nearly dark."

"I can't figure it out that quickly." She was exhausted and hungry. And confused.

"I'll prepare Elvera's room for you." Norman started to turn away.

Esther grabbed hold of his arm. "No. I'll use my old room." There was no way she could sleep up there. For a moment the crackle of fire filled her mind.

"You're staying?" Scarlett asked. "Are you crazy? Break the binding and-"

Jesse interrupted her. "Lady Knight." He took her

hand, smiling at her. "Let others make their own mistakes."

"You think this is a mistake?" Esther let go of Norman to make a vague gesture towards him and the house.

Jesse shrugged. "Only time will tell."

"I'll prepare a meal for you." Norman indicated the three hunters, his gaze remaining on Esther. "Are you dining alone or with company?"

"I don't-" She broke off, her mind reeling. "I have no-" Again she broke off. "This is ridiculous." The words burst from her and she gestured towards the house. "This isn't me."

"We can purchase a house more suited to your tastes," Norman said.

She stared at him. A fortnight ago she was struggling to afford clothes for an interview. Today someone was offering to take her house shopping. "I need sleep." With the way her luck usually went, she'd wake up to find it had been a dream. A strange, confusing dream.

"I'll make a light meal for you while you wash and change into fresh clothes." Norman looked her up and down. "I took the liberty of purchasing ones more suited to what you tend to wear rather than what Elvera requested for you."

She stared after him, her mouth once more hanging open. She closed it, slowly shaking her head as she tried to figure out what was going on and how everything had changed so quickly.

Malachi slipped an arm around her shoulders. "Are you okay?"

"I don't know." She gestured towards the house. "How can any of this be possible?"

"You could donate it all to charities," Scarlett said. "There might be unknown strings to the deal."

"I can go over the paperwork for you if you'd like," Jesse suggested.

Esther drew away from Malachi to face Jesse. "Why? Are you a lawyer?"

"Worse." Jesse grinned. "I used to be a demon. We can outdo lawyers with our ability to create contracts that mean something completely different than you think they do."

She drew in a deep, shaky breath. "Okay." She was so far out of her depth she had no idea what to do next. Normally that proceeded her getting into a fight, but she'd never been in a situation like this. She thought of Nethod and her lips slowly curved into a smile. Maybe she wasn't that far out of her depth after all. If it was one thing she knew, it was how to keep fighting. The daggers hummed, vibrating with life.

It seemed like she wasn't the only one who thought fighting was a good idea.

"You've come to a decision," Malachi said.

Chapter Twenty-Five

Esther met Malachi's gaze, surprised by his comment. More surprised that she thought he might be right. She'd spent her life getting into fights and getting in and out of trouble. Maybe she should stick with what she knew. Her hands curled into fists and she could almost feel the handles of the daggers. "I think I have." Her smile widened into a grin. She hadn't needed to change anything about herself. Had only needed to figure out what it was she should be fighting.

"You're going to become an executioner," Jesse said.

She faced him again, shrugging a single shoulder. "I guess I'll see what happens after I track Nethod down." She glanced at the doorway. "For now, I'm going to have something to eat then sleep."

"I'll remain with you." Malachi turned to Jesse.

"Could you drop my vehicle off here?" He handed over his keys when Jesse nodded. The two clasped hands to arms so their wrists met.

Scarlett did the same before hugging Malachi. "Go with God."

Malachi grinned. "I'll be okay. Mum swears I have a guardian angel watching over me."

Scarlett slowly shook her head, a reluctant smile forming. "She says the guardian angel watching over you must have their work cut out for them."

"There you go, she says I have a guardian angel watching over me."

Scarlett hugged him once more before striding towards the vehicle, Jesse at her side, walking arm in arm.

Esther watched them leave, a wave of wistfulness washing over her. What must it be like to have someone at your side that you could always count on? And they obviously could count on each other. Their actions had clearly shown that.

"Come on." Malachi draped his arm around her shoulders. "You look like you're barely managing to stay upright. Food then bed."

She was too exhausted to protest his comment. She wasn't about to collapse. But the words would have been a lie. She had no idea how she continued to function with how exhausted she was.

Food and getting ready for bed were a blur and she woke hours later to stare at her phone, surprised to find it was nearly midnight. She returned the phone to the bedside cabinet and turned on the light, blinking rapidly at the brightness. A tap on her door drew her attention. She stared at it a moment before she climbed out of bed and crossed the room to cautiously open it.

Norman stood in front of her, his broad shoulders filling the doorway. "If you're hungry there is chicken curry being kept warm for you."

Several sentences half formed before vanishing. He was going to run around after her now? She wasn't sure how she felt about that.

"Do you want me to make something different for you?" Norman asked.

"No. I'll be out shortly." She closed the door, leaning against it and closing her eyes. She should be accustomed to her life being continually out of her control. Her hands curled into fists. That would change. Opening her eyes, she pushed away from the door. She'd been trying to take control of her life for years, fighting against everything in an effort to do so. This time she'd be successful. She felt the tug of the daggers, running her fingers over the mark on her left wrist.

The memory of how powerless she'd felt at her first encounter of demons filled her mind. She'd never feel that way again. Nor would she allow demons to make others feel that way. Straightening her shoulders, she strode to the ensuite. It was time to take back control of her life in the only way she knew how. By fighting for it.

After a quick shower and changing into jeans and a mid-weight long sleeve shirt, she made her way to the dining table. Her steps slowed when she saw Malachi was at the table and that Norman dished up food for the two of them, a bowl for her in front of the seat Elvera had once used.

"Did you want wine with your meal?" Norman asked.

"No." The word burst from her. She started to say she wasn't Elvera and had no plan to take her place in this house or in Norman's life. Instead, she picked up the bowl and shifted it to the seat opposite Malachi. He was in the seat she would normally use. When Norman started to walk away, she took a step towards him. "Do you eat?"

Norman faced her, nodding. "Yes. Like humans, we require sustenance."

"Then grab a bowl and join us." Things would be different. She wasn't Elvera and had no plans to be turned into her.

The meal was mostly silent. Esther had a lot of things to think about. And plans to come up with. Finished eating, she checked her phone. It was after midnight. "I need to learn where Nethod is."

Norman cleared the table. "He won't have gone far. He'll be close enough to watch for the opportunity to destroy you."

Esther rose from the table. "I need a map, candle and herbs."

"Everything you need is upstairs." Norman placed the dirty dishes beside the sink. "I'll show you where it's kept."

Esther looked in the direction of the stairs. "No. I want to do the ritual at the dining table." She really needed a lowset house.

It didn't take Norman long to gather everything Esther needed and set it up on the dining table. He returned to cleaning the kitchen while she did the ritual, Malachi at her side.

She watched a blood drop form on the map. It was three streets away. No other blood drops formed. "How do I know which ones to return to hell and which ones to execute?"

"You will know," Norman said.

"How?" Esther demanded. "And how would you know?"

Norman joined them at the table and rolled his sleeve back enough to show the mark that slashed a quarter of the way across his wrist. "Some things you never forget."

"You were nearly an executioner? You didn't just have the daggers. You actually used them." Esther couldn't drag her gaze from his wrists.

"What happened to prevent you from becoming an executioner?" Malachi asked.

Norman glared at Malachi before returning his attention to Esther. "I was once meant to seek out those who had done unspeakable evil, even by demon standards." Norman rolled his sleeves back into place.

Esther was finally able to meet his gaze. "You were one of the good guys?" It didn't seem possible. "What happened to you?"

"Dazreyella." The word was filled with centuries of bitterness.

"That doesn't mean you have to continue to be one of the bad guys," Esther protested.

"We are shaped by the people in our lives and the circumstances we find ourselves in."

She started to protest Norman's words. It would

have been a lie. She held his gaze a moment before speaking. "And by those not in our lives."

He inclined his head.

Malachi moved closer to the map. "The demon hasn't moved. Shall we see if it's Nethod?"

Esther looked from the map to Norman, eventually nodding.

"Do you want me to accompany you?" Norman asked.

She glanced at his covered wrists. "No." She didn't trust him. He might once have been planning to become an executioner, but he'd taken a different path.

Norman inclined his head. "I understand."

Meeting his gaze, Esther saw that he did understand. For a moment she felt bad for him. The feeling passed as quickly as it arrived. She turned to Malachi. "How soon can you be ready?"

"Give me a minute."

When she nodded, Malachi strode from the room. She started to follow him.

"I have no anger towards you."

She faced Norman. "Would you if you weren't bound to the company?"

Norman shook his head. "As soon as Elvera's hold

wore off, I realised you did me a favour. If anything, I owe you for freeing me from her."

She had no idea what to say. Or do. "I should go."

Norman inclined his head. "Anything you need, all you have to do is tell me and I will make certain you have it."

His offer made her feel uncomfortable, but she nodded anyway, wanting to escape the conversation. She took a step back from him. "I have to go." She fled to the front door before he could speak. Reaching it, she thought of the map she'd left behind. She wasn't about to go back and get it.

Malachi came down the stairs and headed towards her. "I'm ready."

She looked past him. "What was upstairs?"

"Norman let me crash in one of the spare rooms." Malachi grinned. "You learn to sleep when and where you can when you're a hunter." He glanced at her wrist. "If you still plan to do this, you'll learn to do the same."

She thought about it, not going after Nethod and using the executioner daggers on him. It was an almost physical pain, causing her to catch her breath. Drawing in a slow and steady breath, she focused on the thought of going after Nethod. A feeling of rightness flowed through her, like it was in her bloodstream, reaching every part of her body. Including the daggers. She frowned. They were a part of her? A moment of fear struck, rapidly followed by acceptance. This wasn't the same as every other time that control of her life had been taken from her. She had chosen this. The daggers vibrated, the sense of them filling her.

"Is something wrong?" Malachi asked.

She smiled. "No." If anything, something was finally right. No one was ever going to take control of her life again. The crackle of fire echoed in her memory. Or take anyone from her. She had the means to fight for what she wanted. To protect those around her. The daggers and Elvera's estate. And Elvera had inadvertently taught her how the business was run. "Let's go after Nethod."

Malachi nodded, opening the door. "Then we can talk about where we're going on our date."

She followed him through the doorway, about to agree with him. "No." She tugged him back to her, remaining in front of the open front door. "Why wait?" Life was too dangerous to put anything off. She looked up at him. "Tonight. We'll go somewhere tonight."

He stared down at her a moment before grinning. "Dinner and a movie?"

"Yeah." It had been a long time since she'd done anything so normal. Or wanted to do anything so normal. She closed the distance between them, her hand resting on his chest. "That sounds good." Her gaze roamed his face as she wondered if she had to make every move.

"We can argue over the movie during dinner." His arms slid around her waist and he lowered his head, his lips close to hers.

She met his gaze, about to ask him what he was waiting for when his lips met hers. She sank against his body, her hand sliding up to tangle in his hair. She clung to him, his arms tight around her. Eventually, she drew back slightly. A smile slowly formed. "Ready to go after Nethod?"

"I'm always ready to take on demons." He kept an arm around her as they headed for his vehicle.

They were nearly at the location when it struck Esther that she had no idea how to fight with daggers. She was accustomed to fighting with her fists. It was too late now. She ran her hand over one of the sheathed daggers at her ankle. She'd figure it out somehow. Hadn't she managed to take out both Torrnon and Elvera? Nethod didn't stand a chance. She felt the hum of the daggers, as if they agreed with her.

Malachi pulled up in front of a dark, high set building that loomed over them, casting lengthy shadows onto the street. The nearby streetlights were out. "You sure you're up to this?"

"Yeah." She'd make certain of it.

Malachi reached into the back and gathered two sheathed swords, strapping them on once he was out of the vehicle. He headed towards the house when Esther joined him.

She scanned the area. Nothing moved. Everything was silent. "Why is it so quiet?" She whispered the words. It felt wrong to speak aloud.

Malachi shrugged. "Who knows. I noticed there were a few for sale signs in front of some of the houses. More than you'd expect in any single street. Could be a problem with the area."

"Great."

Malachi chuckled. "It is, actually. Should keep humans out of the way."

"What if someone sees us using weapons?"

"We pray they don't call the police." He opened the front door. It swung open easily.

"Think he's waiting for us?" Esther drew two of her daggers, noticing Malachi drew one of his swords.

"He'll know we're here. Or at least a hunter is here. I don't know if he'd be able to sense you. I know as much as you do about executioners. Possibly less than you know." Malachi drew out a small torch, shining the light on the floor before entering the house.

Chapter Twenty-Six

Esther followed Malachi, wishing she had a torch too. But then she wouldn't be able to hold a dagger in each hand.

Malachi led them into a large, empty room. "He's upstairs. Can you sense him?"

She breathed out heavily. "Of course he is."

"Did you want me to go after him?" Malachi asked.

"I can do this." She didn't know if she was trying to convince herself or him. The crackle of flames filled her mind, a memory she'd like to forget. Or at least not remember so clearly.

Light filled the room and two men entered. One of them chuckled. "Put your sword away, boy, or I'll be forced to take out my gun."

Malachi grinned, sheathing his sword and turning off the torch, tucking it into a pocket. "Won't help you any. You might want to draw that gun if you hope to win."

"Are you crazy?" Esther kept her voice low, not wanting the two men to hear her words.

Malachi stepped forward, between Esther and the men. "You go after Nethod. I've got these two."

The second man chuckled. "I do like to see a confident opponent. Makes it more satisfying when I bring them to their knees."

Before Esther could protest again, the three attacked each other. She stumbled back, opening her mouth to tell Malachi to run. She closed her mouth, the words unspoken. With the way he moved, Malachi had good reason to be confident.

"Go on, Esther." Malachi blocked a punch, sinking one of his own into his opponent before dodging away from the other man. "I'll join you soon."

"You might have a few skills," the first man said. "But even you won't be able to outlast us."

"You've got nothing on what I normally fight." Malachi chuckled. "Although I do appreciate the workout. Thanks for that."

Esther reluctantly retreated, looking for the stairs, the sound of fighting and insults being traded, fading. It didn't take her long to find the stairs, the timber tread mostly in shadows. She started to sheath one of her daggers when candles sprang to life on every second step. Her gaze was drawn upwards. A single candle was on the small landing at the top. She tried to swallow. Fear clogged her throat. Her grip tightened on the hilt of the daggers. The fear receded as the hum of the daggers filled her.

She strode up the stairs, candles blinking out as she passed them. She wasn't going fast enough that it would be the air of her passing that put them out. Focusing on the flickering flame at the top of the stairs, she kept going. Nethod wasn't going to scare her with his tricks.

Reaching the top, she knew exactly where to go. The room ahead of her. The door was closed, but swung open as she approached, the last candle going out. Not that it mattered. There were several candles inside the room, Nethod standing in the middle of the floor. She froze in the doorway, her mouth hanging open when she saw the symbols painted on the floor in red, a candle next to each one. A human body was slumped in the corner in a puddle of blood.

"They're dead?" She was relieved none of the shock and fear sounded in her tone.

Nethod shrugged. "He's working on it." He formed a sword. "I wonder who will die first. You or him."

She forced herself to stride towards Nethod. "Neither. It will be you." How long did Nethod's victim have? Did she have time to save him? Determined to take Nethod out before the human died, she attacked, slashing at Nethod with one of her daggers while blocking with the other. Even though she was accustomed to using fists in a fight there was a certain familiarity about fighting with the daggers. Like they were a part of her. Again the sense of them hummed through her. Maybe they were.

"Torrnon was my brother in every sense of the word. Born of the same mother and father. You will pay in pain and blood for what you did to him." Nethod fought back, his sword moving quickly.

Esther had no idea how she managed to avoid being struck by the sword. Several times she made slashing cuts across Nethod's skin, blood welling. But it wasn't enough. Somehow she had to make him consume her blood for the daggers to work properly.

"I know about you," Nethod said. "I know your past. And I know how you will end. The same way your family did."

"You know nothing." She fought harder, the daggers slicing random patterns of blood across his body. "Nothing." The smoky scent of Nethod had her struggling not to think of that night.

"There were flames filling the staircase. A beam pinned your father. No one could reach them. I found witnesses. They said you ran screaming into the night. That you deserted them."

She drew in a sharp breath as his sword cut flesh, blood welling on her arm, soaking her sleeve. "They told me to run." She yelled the words at him.

"You won't be able to run this time." Nethod grinned, blocking her attack. "You'll go the same way they went." Flames rose up around them, encircling them.

The scent of smoke and the crackle of fire filled her senses. Her initial reaction was to run. She saw it in Nethod's expression that he expected her to try. A sense of calm filled her. She'd known this moment was long overdue. They'd told her so many times that it had been a miracle she'd escaped. A miracle she'd lived. Miracles obviously had an expiry date. "You're going to have to try better than this." She wasn't a terrified little kid listening to screams piercing the night, her own replacing them when they'd fallen silent. Her grip tightened on the daggers. "You will join your brother." She'd make sure she wasn't the only one to die. Nethod would die too. And if the human in the corner was lucky, Malachi would discover him before he died and call for help.

Nethod's attacks slowed. "I discovered everything about you."

She grinned at the uncertainty in his voice. "Obviously not." She slashed at him, slamming her arm against his mouth when he stumbled back. Pain shot through her as her blood entered his system. Then it struck again. A burning, slashing sensation around her wrists. She didn't need to look. She knew.

Nethod's eyes widened. "Executioner." He said the word like it was a curse.

She inclined her head. "Yes." There was no hesitation. She'd found something worth fighting for. She glanced at the body in the corner. She understood now. Better than Nethod understood anything. "I'd ask you to give your brother a message from me, but I understand once your ties are severed from all existence, there's nothing." She threw herself at Nethod, knocking him to the floor, plunging a dagger into him.

He moved enough to avoid a mortal wound, roaring when the dagger pierced him. The flames around them rose, drawing closer. "I will take you with me." His arms closed around her.

She didn't fight him, letting him pull her onto him, the second dagger poised to pierce his body, drawing the first one from him. "I doubt it." Her face was close to his. She wasn't about to give him the satisfaction of thinking he could win in any way.

He crushed her to him, his arms tightening as he roared when the second dagger pierced his body.

She pushed the dagger in deeper. It was impossible for her to draw it out as it was crushed between the two of them. It was also beginning to become impossible for her to breathe. She ran the first dagger across his throat, blood welling up, splattering her face. His grip didn't loosen. She sliced at him again and again. The world faded around the edges, her breathing laboured. The heat of the flames made sweat drip down her face, mingling with the blood. "Die damn you." The words were a forced whisper.

Nethod opened his mouth to speak. No words formed. The flames burned lower and his grip finally loosened.

She was able to draw the second dagger out. She'd barely removed it when she was engulfed in flames, Nethod's body consumed by them. Rolling out of the way, she slapped at her smouldering clothes, landing on her back to stare up at the ceiling.

Running footsteps coming up the stairs had her trying to struggle to her feet. Pain exploded through her and she dropped back. The room was dim, only the candles burning, the flames extinguished now

Nethod was gone. She groaned as she tried to get to her feet again. The human in the corner needed help.

Malachi appeared above her, reaching for her. He drew back before he could make contact. "Don't move. I'll call for medical help."

"I'm okay." She struggled to sit up again. "He's the one who needs medical help." She gestured to the corner with one of her daggers.

Malachi, who'd taken out his phone, glanced in the direction, taking a second look. "Don't move and I'll check on him." He raised the phone to his ear as he strode to the human. "Urgent medical help needed." He knelt beside the still body as he explained the situation.

Esther stopped trying to rise from the floor. Everything ached. The scent of burnt flesh and wood filled her senses. For once they didn't fill her with fear. She'd won. The hum of the daggers sang through her. They'd won. Her and the daggers.

It didn't take long before medical help arrived. And it wasn't an ambulance like Esther had expected. Once the doctor gave her the all clear to move, she walked downstairs with Malachi, his arm around her waist. She glanced over her shoulder. "Will he be okay? The one Nethod tried to kill."

"Nethod didn't try and kill him. He needed the blood."

Luca strode towards them, Penelope at his side. "I hear you made a mess for us to clean up."

Malachi chuckled at Luca's words. "It wasn't me this time." He looked down at Esther. "It was the demon executioner."

She stared up at him, the words ringing through her. A smile slowly formed. "Yeah. And I plan to do it again."

Malachi grinned as he fully faced her, his other arm going around her. "Is that an invitation?"

She laughed.

Before she could answer, Luca spoke. "Doesn't matter if it isn't. If there's trouble, Malachi will be there."

Esther wrapped her arms around Malachi. "That's what they've always said about me."

Penelope laughed, turning to Luca. "No wonder Malachi was drawn to her. I actually feel the slightest bit of pity for any demons they go after." She started for the stairs.

Malachi continued to meet Esther's gaze, his words directed to Penelope and Luca. "Photograph the symbols Nethod made. Gran will want to know what he was up to." He grinned. "And keep your pity for those who need it. Because it won't be any demons we go after."

Esther returned his grin. "No, if we go after demons, it will be because they deserve everything coming to them."

"Exactly." Malachi's arms tightened around her before his lips met hers.

She clung to him, ignoring the aches and pains of her body. She was alive. And not only alive. Drawing back, she met his gaze again. She'd finally figured things out. There was nothing wrong with fighting. She'd just been fighting the wrong fights. That would change. The hum of the daggers filled her as she drew Malachi's head down, her lips again meeting his. And she knew exactly where the next fight would take her. She could feel it in her like a compass point. She felt a tug from the direction of the Gold Coast. But it could wait. It was time to celebrate her first victory. She was certain there'd be many more to come.

Free Ebook

Subscribe to Avril's newsletter and receive a free ebook. This ebook is exclusive to those on her mailing list. To find out more about this offer visit:

www.avrilsabine.com/free-ebook

*

We value your privacy and will not sell, rent, exchange or loan your email address to third parties. Your information is confidential and you are under no obligation to remain on the mailing list and can unsubscribe at any time.

Acknowledgements

As always, thank you to all the usual crew and a special thanks to Storm and Clint who helped with cover props. And to those of you who figured it out, yes, you are right. Esther is the unnamed character at the end of Demon Hunters 5: Cursed.

To The Reader

If you enjoyed this book, why not consider leaving a review to help other readers discover it too? Reader engagement is one of the few ways that lets an author know readers want more books in a particular series or genre. So leave a review and tell friends, not only about this book but also about other ones you've enjoyed, so you can continue to enjoy books by your favourite authors for years to come.

Dreams are meant to be lived,

Avril.

About The Author

Avril is an Australian author who lives with her family on acreage in South East Queensland. She writes mostly young adult and children's speculative fiction, but has been known to dabble in other genres. You can find more information about her at www.avrilsabine.com where you can also subscribe to her newsletter to be kept informed about new releases, current projects, blog posts and exclusive news.

Titles By Avril Sabine

Stories about strong characters and characters who discover their strengths.

SERIES

Assassins Of The Dead- Young Adult Fantasy/ Paranormal

Book 1: Dark Blade

Book 2: Dragon Touched

Book 3: Society Against Vampires

Book 4: King's Request

Dragon Blood- Young Adult Urban Fantasy (with elements of romance)

(5 book series)

Book 1: Pliethin

Book 2: Wyvern

Book 3: Surety

Book 4: Knight

Book 5: Mage

Dragon Mage- Young Adult Urban Fantasy (with elements of romance)

(Series two of Dragon Blood series)

Book 1: Promise

Dragon Blood Chronicles- Young Adult Urban Fantasy (with elements of romance)

(Companion stand alone series to Dragon Blood)

Book 1: Oath

Book 2: Betrayed

Guardians Of The Round Table- Young Adult Fantasy LitRPG

(Co-written with Storm and Rhys Petersen)

Book 1: Dexterity Fail

Book 2: Goblin Boots

Book 3: Singed Feathers

Book 4: Frog Mage

Book 5: Crystal Mine

Book 6: Cursed Harp

Rosie's Rangers- Young Adult Western Steampunk

(6 book series)

Book 1: Justice

Book 2: Vengeance

Book 3: Treachery

Book 4: Accused

Book 5: Wanted

Book 6: Corruption

Mark Of Kings- Children's Fantasy

(Upper middle grade/preteen)

(4 book series)

Book 1: The Arena

Book 2: The Island

Book 3: The Assassin

Book 4: The King

STAND ALONE SERIES

Demon Hunters- Young Adult Urban Fantasy/ Horror (with elements of romance)

Book 1: Blood Sacrifice

Book 2: Retribution

Book 3: Tainted

Book 4: Premonition

Book 5: Cursed

Book 6: Feud

Book 7: Extrication

Plea Of The Damned- Young Adult Urban Fantasy/Paranormal

(6 book series)

Book 1: Forgive Me Lucy

Book 2: Forgive Me Aiden

Book 3: Forgive Me Jena

Book 4: Forgive Me Kobe

Book 5: Forgive Me Marti

Book 6: Forgive Me Dawson

Realms Of The Fae- Young Adult Urban Fantasy (with elements of romance)

The Sword (short story in Like A Girl Anthology)

Heart Of Stone

Book 1: A Debt Owed

Book 2: Marked By The Hunt

Book 3: The Magic Collector

Book 4: An Unexpected Betrayal

Book 5: Imprisoned By Iron

Fairytales Retold (Short Stories)

Snow-White And Rose-Red

The Twelve Brothers

The Light Princess

Beauty And The Beast

Sleeping Beauty

Aschenputtel

The Golden Bird

The Frog Prince

The Death Of Koshchei The Deathless

Myths And Legends Retold (Short Stories)

Ion, Son Of Apollo

Sir Gawain And The Maid With The Narrow Sleeves

Princess Ilse, The Giant's Daughter

YOUNG ADULT NOVELS

Young Adult Fantasy (with elements of romance)

Elf Sight

Earth Bound

Young Adult Urban Fantasy

Stone Warrior (with elements of romance)

The Jungle Inside

Young Adult Contemporary (with elements of romance)

Through Your Eyes

The Ugly Stepsister

Perfect Little Princess

Young Adult Contemporary/Paranormal

Whispers In The Dark (with elements of romance and same sex relationships)

Over Too Soon (with elements of romance)

Young Adult Sci-Fi

Experiment X-One-Six (Urban Sci-Fi/Superheroes)

An Endless Dawn (Post Apocalyptic Sci-Fi)

CHILDREN'S BOOKS

Dragon Lord (Preteen/early teens) (Fantasy)

The Irish Wizard (Upper middle grade) (Urban Fantasy)

SHORT STORIES

Urban Fantasy

Eternally Late

Dealings With Joe

Glimpses (short story in That Moment When Anthology)

Contemporary

The Brat Next Door

Fantasy LitRPG

(Set in the same world as Guardians Of The Round Table Series)

Tales Of Inadon 1: The Disc (Co-written with Storm and Rhys Petersen) (short story in Game On! Anthology)

Post Apocalyptic Sci-Fi

Compulsive Directive

NONFICTION

A Year Of Weekly Writing Exercises (Creative Writing)

Cooking For Families With Allergies (Cooking) (Co-written with Storm Petersen)

Tell Me A Story, Grandma (Memoir)

For the most up to date details on available titles visit:

www.avrilsabine.com/books/bibliography

Demon Hunter Series

To learn more about this series visit:

www.avrilsabine.com/series/dh

BOOKS AVAILABLE IN THE DEMON HUNTER SERIES

Book 1: Blood Sacrifice

Book 2: Retribution

Book 3: Tainted

Book 4: Premonition

Book 5: Cursed

Book 6: Feud

Book 7: Extrication

Disclaimer

This is a work of fiction. Names, characters, businesses, places, events and incidents are either the products of the author's imagination or used in a fictitious manner. Any resemblance to actual persons, living or dead, or actual events is purely coincidental. The opinions expressed or beliefs held are those of the characters and should not be assumed to be the opinions or beliefs of the author.